KINGS OF THE BLOCK:

THE WILLIAMS BROTHERS

DWAN WILLIAMS

GOOD 2 GO PUBLISHING

KINGS OF THE BLOCK: THE WILLIAMS BROTHERS

Written by Dwan Williams

Cover Design: Davida Baldwin – Odd Ball Designs

Typesetter: Mychea

ISBN: 9781947340350

Copyright © 2019 Good2Go Publishing

Published 2019 by Good2Go Publishing

7311 W. Glass Lane • Laveen, AZ 85339

www.good2gopublishing.com

https://twitter.com/good2gobooks

G2G@good2gopublishing.com

www.facebook.com/good2gopublishing

www.instagram.com/good2gopublishing

KINGS OF THE BLOCK:

THE WILLIAMS BROTHERS

This book is dedicated to my great grandmother (R.I.P.) Georgiana Williams-Barnes, G-Babies Jah-Ceon Moore, Alayah Neely, and Amir Neely. Also, to my family and everyone that has supported me and read my work! GOD Bless you all!!!!

Acknowledgments

I would like to thank a very good friend of mine, Harold Hall Jr., for the endless days and night helping me with the project. Words can't begin to express how grateful I am to have you as a real friend. A special thanks goes out to Kimberly and Danshauna Floyd for all of the love and support they have shown/given me throughout the years.

I would also like to thank Philip Witherspoon, Mike Wells, my cousins Erica Williams and Torey Barnes for holding me down throughout the years and my niece Arnessia Williams.

I would like to acknowledge mt people on lock that have shown their support. I will only name a few because if I name you all, this would end up a book in itself. Watkita "The Prince" Valenzuela, Jerry Partee, Frog, Fred Cloud, Hasan "Jersey" Williams, Vegas, Charles Rice, Dashuan "K-Yown" King, Rico "Polo" Moses, Demarcus "Nelly" Baxter, Michael Lawrence, Mike & Johan farmer and my entire Wide-A-Wake family.

Last but not least, I would like to acknowledge G2G for giving me this platform to showcase my work od art.

1

HOW IT ALL STARTED

RIINNNGGGG!!! Marquis was snapped out of his daydream by the sound of the three o'clock school bell. He glanced up and around as all the other kids headed to the front of the class to the teacher's desk. He gathered his things and then did the same to get his report card. "Congratulations, Marquis," Mrs. Jones said with a smile on her face.

Mrs. Jones was his last period teacher. She was about twenty years older than him, but that didn't stop him from daydreaming about her every day. He secretly had a crush on her; he paid attention to every detail about her when she would stand in front of the class and teach her lessons. The way Mrs. Jones's big round breasts protruded through her blouse kept him in a trance. Not to mention the way her phat hips and ass threatened to burst out of the seams of whatever she wore to try to conceal them, made him have plenty of wet dreams.

"Thanks, Mrs. Jones," he replied, returning a smile. He opened it on the spot to see what it read even though he already knew that he had passed his grade. He kept all As in every subject besides physical education, in which he made

Cs. He wasn't really into sports, but the main problem he had was he didn't have any extra clothes to change into to participate in the activities like the other kids.

When he read his report card, it confirmed what he knew. He had passed his grade and would be entering his freshman year in high school. "So, Marquis, what are your plans for the summer?"

As the last student exited the classroom, he answered, "I plan on getting a summer job and helping my mother out around the house with my brother and sister." His smile slowly faded after he responded. His family not having things was always a soft spot for him. He constantly thought about how his mother would struggle from day to day to keep food on the table and clothes on their backs. She would do whatever she had to do to provide for her family. This year would be the first year that he would be able to get a work permit and take some of the weight off of his mother's shoulders, and that's exactly what he planned on doing, no matter what odd jobs he had to do. Mrs. Jones's heart warmed as she saw the sincerity in his eyes.

"That's so sweet of you," she replied as she gently pinched his jaw. "I hope you find a good job." She stood to her feet and walked around to the front of her desk where he was standing. At that very moment Marquis closed his eyes and prayed one of his daydreams was about to finally come true. He opened them when he heard her speak again. "Well since you'll be in high school next year I guess I won't be seeing you anymore. I want you to know that you were always my favorite student." A smile suddenly reappeared on his face after hearing those words. "Marquis, no matter what you decide to do in life. I want you to always do your best, and I know you will succeed." She looked him dead in his eyes letting him know she truly believed in him.

"I will," he promised.

"And I want you to keep Alexander out of trouble." They both started laughing as Marquis looked at her and raised one eyebrow.

Alexander was Marquis's brother. Even though he was younger, he was much bigger than Marquis. People often thought that Alexander was the oldest. He stayed in some kind of trouble, and Marquis was always brought into the middle of it. Alexander was a good kid but ended up in a lot of fights because the other kids would sometimes tease him about his clothes or old run-over shoes.

"I'll do my best," he replied as he put his report card in the old book bag that he had for the past three school years. He headed toward the door and then took one last look back at Mrs. Jones, snapping a picture into his mental

Rolodex, knowing it would be his last time seeing her.

As soon as he walked out of the class, his brother was standing beside the door waiting on him. "What took you so long?" Alexander asked as they headed down the hall.

"Chill, you know I had to say good-bye to my lady," Marquis joked, and they both burst in laughter. Alexander knew Marquis had a thing for Mrs. Jones even though he'd never admit it to anybody. They made it to the front of the school where Nicole was waiting on them.

Nicole was their sister. She was the youngest of them all, and they treated here just as that, the baby. She was very cute and developing at a fast rate. She was also very smart but had few friends because of the way she dressed. She did the best with what she had, even though that wasn't much.

On the way home, they had to walk past the arcade. The arcade was the hangout spot all the cool kids would go to after school to play games, get a bite to eat, or just shoot the shit. If you were hip, that was the place to be.

Marquis slowed down a little as he looked through the front window of the arcade. Alexander and Nicole noticed their brother and slowed down as well to see what had caught his attention. "Go over and talk to her," Nicole suggested when she realized who Marquis was looking at. Just when he was about to turn around and walk away, their eyes met. He wanted to look away but was captured by her beauty. To his surprise she began to wave and head in his direction. His heart dropped to the pit of his stomach as he took a deep swallow to get the lump out of his throat. He looked around to make sure she was waving at him and then shyly waved back. He didn't really know what he was going to say to her once she approached him since he had never spoken to her before and this was her first time even acknowledging he existed.

"Come on, Nicole, let's go play Ms. Pac-Man." Alexander reached into his pocket and pulled out two quarters and handed her one. As they made their way through the arcade door, Marquis walked also but was quickly met by Tosha.

Tosha was one of the prettiest girls at his school. She stayed dressed in all the latest designer clothes and wore a hand and neck full of jewelry. At five foot nine, with brown skin, a phat ass, and C-cup sized breasts, she definitely was top of the line, she was very fit due to the fact that she was the head cheerleader for the past two years in a row. Word was that next year when she entered high school she was going to be the head cheerleader for the varsity football team.

"Hello, your name is Marquis, correct?" Tosha asked sounding much older than she actually was.

"Y-Y-Yes," he stuttered. She smiled as she noticed how nervous he was acting from being in her presence. She was used to that effect she had on most guys, but she liked the shyness Marquis was showing.

"That's correct." He had no idea where the words came from, but he was glad they came out. He didn't want Tosha to think he was a weirdo or something. She stretched her arm out in his direction to shake his hand. He wiped the sweat from his palm and placed it in hers.

"You were in my math class this year. You're

very smart. Maybe you can teach me a thing or two in that subject." He agreed, and just like that they became cool. They were deep in conversation before they got interru-pted by some people arguing in the back of the arcade. He directed his attention to the noise and noticed that Alexander was standing face-to-face with the bully of their school (Big Curt) and two of his friends (Quick and Nitty).

"Excuse me for a minute please," Marquis told Tosha as he made his way up to the crowd of people. Nicole was standing behind Alexander with tears in her eyes her begging him to come on. Marquis stood off to the side to see if anything was going to pop off. Alexander looked up and saw his brother and immediately

stole Big Curt in his nose, breaking it on impact.

Big Curt let out a muffled moan as he grabbed

his bloodied nose and hit the ground. Big Curt's

friend Quick tried to rush Alexander, but Marquis

caught him from his blind side with a two-piece

combination to his jaw, dropping him instantly.

Quick got the name for his swiftness around the

boxing ring, but at that moment all his boxing

skills were out the door. All he could do now was

ball up in the fetal position and try to block as

many of the punches as he could to survive.

Before the other friend, Nitty, could jump in to

help his partners, Alexander caught him with a

right hook to his eye. Nitty spun around on his

heel from the vicious blow and jetted out of the arcade, leaving his friends to fend for themselves.

"Beat dat nigga's ass," Alexander cheered as his brother went to work. Quick was saved by Old Man John, the arcade manager, as he came from the back full speed with a bat in hand yelling for the fight to break up. Alexander pulled Marquis off of Quick and ran out of the arcade with Nicole dead on their heels behind them.

When they made it down the street they stopped running and tried to catch their breath. "Yo, what was all that about back there?" Marquis asked Alexander as he bent over with both hands on his knees.

"It was all my fault," Nicole cut in as she lowered her head toward the pavement. She didn't want Marquis to put the blame on Alexander.

"No, it wasn't your fault," Alexander assured her. "That bitch-ass nigga had no business touching your butt in the first place. He lucky his nose is the only thing I broke."

"He what?" Marquis shouted as he turned around ready to go back and finish what they started. At that point he didn't care about the manager of the arcade nor if the other guys had regrouped or not. His sister was his heart, and he would die to protect her.

"Please don't," Nicole begged as she

grabbed Marquis by his arm with both of her hands. He paused and turned toward his sister and looked her in the eyes. "Please," she cried out once more. It hurt him even more to see her cry.

"Come on, Bruh," Alexander told Marquis as he threw his arm around his shoulder and pulled him along. "Your right almost looked as good as mine back there," Alexander joked. Marquis threw a quick right hook followed by a left cross in his brother's direction. Alexander sidestepped it with ease and then threw his guard up.

"Aight!" Alexander warned as he got low in a defensive stance.

"Y'all come on," Nicole said impatiently,

looking around to make sure that no one was following them.

~ ~ ~

Nicole walked a few steps ahead of her brothers as they talked boy talk.

"I can't believe that we are out for the entire summer," Marquis boasted as they made a right on Bragg Street.

"Me either," Alexander agreed since he didn't have to attend summer school like he did the two previous summers. "Now I can sleep all day if I want to!"

Nicole glanced back at her brothers and shook her head.

"I know that's right." Marquis laughed and

then gave his brother a high five. Before they could say another word, a voice could be heard from someone across the street that sat on the porch of a well-known trap house.

"Damn, shorty got a phat ass on her," one of the hustlers shouted from the front porch of the trap house he was selling drugs from.

"You ain't lying," his partner looked up and admitted and then stood to his feet.

"Come on, y'all, just keep walking," Nicole tried to persuade her brothers, but it was no use. Alexander had already turned around, and Marquis was right on his heels. Nicole closed her eyes and said a quick, silent prayer then stood and watched things play out.

"What you just say about my little sister?"
Alexander questioned as he stood in front of the
trap house with Marquis by his side. Even
though they were outnumbered two to three,
Alexander felt like after he knocked the big one
out, he and Marquis could easily take the other
two one on one.

"You hear this nigga, Big Kev?" D.J. turned
and looked at his partner. Big Kev cracked his
knuckles as he pushed D.J. to the side and
headed down the steps. He wasn't into much lip
boxing; he let his hands do the talking for him.
Big Kev and Alexander stood face-to-face,
waiting for the other to make a move. Before a
single punch could be thrown, Rodney stood up

from his spot on the porch and spoke.

"Stand down," he ordered Big Kev and D.J. Being that he was a little older, not to mention the big homie, his voice carried a lot of weight with them. Big Kev took a few steps back but never took his gaze off of Alexander.

"What's the problem?" Rodney asked.

"These niggas—" Big Kev began, but Rodney held up his hand to silence him.

"I'm not talking to you!" Big Kev took two steps back and continued to grill Alexander.

"Your boy got slick out of his mouth and disrespected my lil sister," Alexander answered, grilling Big Kev back. Rodney looked up and across the street to Nicole standing by herself.

Nicole nervously looked away and began fiddling with her hair.

"Which boy?" Rodney asked, bringing his attention back to the situation at hand. After following Alexander's stare, Rodney commanded Big Kev to him.

"Apologize to the young lady," he ordered. Big Kev looked from Rodney to Nicole in disbelief.

"But!—"

"Now!" Rodney shouted.

"I'm sorry, shorty," Big Kev held his head down and mumbled.

"Come on y'all," Nicole pleaded from across the street after breathing a sigh of relief. Marquis

21

and Alexander backpedaled until they were a few houses down from the spot.

On the way home, they all thought of the events that had taken place throughout the day. Marquis thought of Tosha and their conversation at the arcade before they got into it with Speedy, Nitty, and Quick. Alexander thought of a way to get at Big Kev and his partners, while Nicole thought about Rodney and the way he looked at her when he thought no one was paying attention.

2

EVERYDAY STRUGGLE

As they approached their apartment build-
ing, Marquis noticed Ty and two of his workers,
Kessey and Jun-Bug, propped up on the side of
Ty's new E300 Benz.

Ty was the neighborhood drug dealer. He
always stayed dressed in all the latest
designers, like Polo, Tommy, Nautica, and
Girbaud. He never wore the same thing more
than twice, not even his shoes.

Kessey and Jun-Bug were his two workers,

most would say his two flunkies. You could tell
by Jun-Bug's name what his position in the crew
was. Kessey name should've been kissy, the
way he always kissed Ty's ass. He was a real
live yes-man.

On the way up the steps Ty called out to
Marquis. "Yo, Mark." Alexander and Nicole went
ahead into their apartment.

"What up, Ty?" Marquis asked once he
turned around and headed back down the steps.
He wondered what Ty wanted since he never
spoke to him before. He didn't even know how
Ty knew his name. Kessey and Jun-Bug sat on
the steps to give them some privacy.

"What's up, kid?" They shook hands and

embraced to show love. Marquis felt like he was cool for the first time in his life just being in Ty's presence. He looked around hoping that someone from school would see him so that they could run and tell somebody that knew somebody that they saw him chilling with the infamous Ty, but it was just his luck that no one was around. "So today was the last day of school, huh?" Marquis bobbed his head up and down and then waited for him to continue. "So, what you gonna do for the summer?" It was like that was the million-dollar question everyone seemed to want to know the answer to that day.

"I don't know," Marquis responded. "I was thinking about going over to McDonald's to get a job, so I could help my mother out around the house," he proudly announced with a smile on his face. Ty looked into his eyes and shook his head from side to side.

"McDonald's!" Ty repeated with a slight chuckle as if Marquis had just told him a joke. "You can't stack no paper like this at no McDonald's." Ty reached in his two front pockets and pulled out stacks of fifties and hundreds and waved them in Marquis's face. Marquis's eyes grew wide, and he wondered what he had to do to get money like Ty had. "You must not intend on helping ma dukes out much if you think McDonald's going to pay you enough to make a difference! Besides, what

KINGS OF THE BLOCK

bitch in her right mind will brag about her man

working in a fast-food restaurant?" Ty contin-

ued. As soon as those words escaped his lips

Marquis's mind went back to the arcade, then to

all the fun him and Tosha would have together

if he had that kind of money.

"So, what do I got to do to get money like

that?" Marquis asked as he pointed to the wad

of money Ty still had out in his hands. "'Cause

I'm not trying to rob or hurt anybody."

Marquis let him know up front to make sure

they had an understanding of things. Ty smiled

as he pictured the little nerdy-looking kid

attempting to rob someone.

"Nah, kid, if I wanted a hitman I would've

stopped your brother and hollered at him. This shit here that I'm putting on the table requires brains. You have to be smart to survive, and I've been watching you throughout the year, and I like how you move."

"The way I move," Marquis thought to himself as he looked down at his legs. He thought he moved the same as any kid around his way.

"In silence and alone." Marquis shook his head up and down now realizing what Ty meant by his comment. "If you keep it that way you'll be the best at what you do." That was the second time that day that someone said that to him, so he figured that it had to be true. "Then maybe you'll become the big man like me."

Marquis sucked in every word Ty spoke. The

more he listened, the more eager he became.

"All you have to do is take a package from point

A to point B, and I'll give you $500 a pop, that

simple." Marquis's heart began to beat out of

control. It sounded really easy, and the fact that

he never had that much money of his own in his

life or even seen that much at one time, made

him want to do it even more. To make that much

money took his mother two weeks and a few

hours of overtime. He knew with that kind of

money his family would never have to struggle

again. He didn't want to seem too anxious to

take Ty's offer, so he told him that he would let

him know his decision by the end of the week. Before Marquis walked away to go into his apartment building Ty had called out to him.

"What's this for?" Marquis asked as Ty handed him a hundred-dollar bill.

"This just a little something to get you some kicks or to take you a little honey out," Ty replied as Marquis took it out of his hand and put it in his pocket and headed up the steps. Before he went into the apartment, he looked back, and Ty and his two flunkies were getting in his Benz and then jetted off down the block.

When he went into the apartment, he found Carolyn in the kitchen stirring a pot of beans and rice.

Carolyn was a proud single mother in her thirties. She worked a full-time job during the week and a ten-hour job on the weekends at her second job, to provide for her family. She always made sure ends met. She was very strict on her children. She wanted all of them to get a good education, so they could succeed in the cruel world that they lived in. She didn't want them to go through life as she did, especially Nicole. That's why she kept her the closest to her.

"Hi, Mother." Marquis's face always lit up seeing the beauty his mother possessed.

"Hi, Marquis, your brother and sister told me what happened today after school," she told him while never taking her eyes off of what she was cooking. His smile slowly crept from his face as his chin met his chest. He knew he was in for a tongue-lashing because his mother was a godly woman and brought them up on turning the other cheek. What came out of her mouth next made him lift his head up. "I am very proud of you, Son. Never let any man disrespect your sister." He let out a sigh of relief. "Now go wash your hands because dinner will be ready in a few minutes." Before he did, he walked over to his mother and tapped her on her back. "What is it?" she asked as she turned toward him.

"I got something I want you to have." He reached in his pocket and pulled out the hundred-dollar bill Ty had just given him. "I found this today and I want you to have it." Her eyes became glassy as she thought of how her oldest son would give her his last to make her happy.

"No, Marquis, it's yours." She bent over and gave him a kiss on his forehead. "Now go wash your hands," she told him as she quickly turned back around while trying to keep Marquis from seeing a tear roll down her face that she was longing to hold back.

He exited the kitchen and snuck into her room to hide the money under her pillow. Marquis knew that his mom would be too proud to take the money from him, but he wasn't taking no for an answer. He then went into the

33

bathroom where his brother and sister were already preparing for dinner and did the same.

They sat around the table and then said their grace and began to eat. Marquis just shook his head as he thought about the four nights out of the week that they sat at the table and ate beans and rice. His mom would sometimes switch up the beans from black-eyed peas to navy beans, but to Marquis, they all tasted the same. He was tired of the everyday struggle his mom had to go through for their family. Ty's offer was becoming more and more tempting by the minute. "What's wrong, Marquis? You've barely touched your food," Carolyn asked looking at his full plate. He hated to lie to his mother, but he didn't want to hurt her feelings by telling her the truth, because

he knew that she did the best she could.

"It's nothing. I'm just a little tired. That's all,"

he told her as he picked up a spoonful of beans

and rice and swallowed them, "I'm not really

hungry. Is it okay if I excuse myself from the

table?"

"Sure, Son, I'll wrap your food up for you and

save it for later." He got up from the table and

went into the bedroom he and Alexander

shared.

Their room was a very small room. The twin-

sized bed they shared, a small chest that sat at

the foot of it, and a stack of milk crates that held

their 13-inch television up was the only thing

that occupied the space.

As soon as he walked in, he snagged his shirt on the clothes hanger that they used for an antenna for the T.V. "Damn," he cursed himself for ruining one of his good shirts. Marquis wanted so bad to be one of the cool kids and fit in with the in crowd around his way, but he knew with only three pairs of pants that he shared with his brother, that was not an option he had. Luckily for him one of the pairs of pants was reversible, making it seem like they had more than they actually did.

Shortly after Alexander walked into their room and lay at the opposite end of the bed. They both lay there for a while on their backs with their hands behind their heads and stared at the ceiling. "So, Bruh, what's really on your mind?" Alexander asked. "And don't come with dat bullshit, 'I'm tired,' that you just ran on Mama, because I know you better than that and I'm not going for it." Marquis took a deep breath before he broke it down.

"You remember earlier when we came home from school and Ty called me over to his car?"

"Yes, I remember. What did he want?"

"Well he told me he wanted to know if I was interested in delivering packages for him." Alexander quickly sat up and looked in his brother's direction.

"So, what you tell 'em?" Marquis could see

the excitement in his brother's eyes. He was excited too but didn't want to show it just yet.

"I told him dat I would let him know my decision by the end of the week." They sat in silence for a few minutes lost in their own thoughts. Alexander was the first to break the silence.

"If you do decide to do it, I want you to know that I want in." Marquis was glad to hear that because he knew if he did take the offer, he was going to need the muscle, and also someone he could really trust. His options for that were limited being he had no friends.

"No doubt." They showed each other some love and lay back down. "This is going to change our lives forever," Marquis said out loud as they went into their own little world thinking about what they were going to do with the money they were going to make. Marquis smiled as his mind drifted to earlier at the arcade when he was with Tosha. "I'm going to make her mine," he said to himself as he closed his eyes.

Nicole flopped down on top of her bed, crossed her arms across her firm breast, and then fell backward into the stuffed animals. She grabbed a Care Bear and kissed it on the lips. "Thank you, Rodney." She blushed as if the bear was him. She didn't know what it was about him, but every time she saw him, between her legs would get moist. Even though Nicole had never had a boyfriend, she knew that she wanted Rodney to be hers. She didn't know how that was going to be, considering the fact that Marquis and Alexander never let her out of their sight. There is one thing that she did know, and that was she was going to find a way to see him, alone. Until then, she was going to continue to have thoughts of him in her mind. Nicole slowly slid her right hand south into her loose shorts and began to touch herself. Her heart sank deep. Today felt different. She began to feel a tingling sensation between her legs for the first time. That's when it happened. She started trembling out of control. She trembled until she removed her hand from between her legs.

That's when she saw it, cum. "I'm a woman now," she gloated, then balled up in a fetal position in the middle of her bed and dozed off to sleep.

3

MOVING ON UP

"Sorry, kid, we're looking for someone with a little experience." That was the third rejection for the day and the seventh one for the week. He walked out of the corner store with his head down and headed back to his apartment building. Marquis was slowly losing hope as each day passed by. "I never knew that finding a job would be this hard," he thought as he began kicking rocks to the side.

He decided to take a shortcut and walked

through the park. It was crowded for a Saturday

morning. Kids were playing on swings, swinging

on monkey bars, whirling on the merry-go-

round, and waiting patiently in line for the guard

to open the gate to the free pool. He noticed a

lot of the new faces were kids from out of town

that came to visit their families for the summer.

As he proceeded up the street, he looked up

then down the block looking at all the local

hustlers on the corners and how all the sexiest

chicks walked by almost naked trying to gain

their attention. All that kept playing through his

mind were the words Ty said to him: "All you

have to do is take a package from point A to

point B, and I'll pay you $500 a pop each time,

that simple." At that very moment he made up his mind that he was going to give it a try.

As soon as he turned the corner to his block, the first thing he saw was Ty leaning on the side of his Champagne-colored Benz talking on his cell phone. He figured now was a perfect time to see if Ty's offer was still on the table for him. When Marquis stopped in front of him to see what was up, Ty held up his pointer finger indicating for Marquis to give him a second for him to handle his business. "So you gonna swallow this time or what?" Ty asked whoever was on the other end. A second later a smile spread across his lips. "That's wassup. I'll be by to pick you up after I leave the club tonight. You better be up too!" he told the caller before hanging up. He placed his cell back on his hip and then directed his attention to Marquis. "So, what's good with you, kid?" They gave each other a pound.

"I was wondering, umm." Marquis looked down at the pavement to try to find the words he was looking for. Ty put his finger under Marquis's chin to lift his head up.

"Always look a man in his eyes when you're talking to him. He'll respect you more for that. That's your first lesson," Ty told him as he removed his finger. Marquis nodded his head in understanding as Ty finished off the question for him. "So, you ready to step up?"

"No doubt," Marquis responded full of confidence as he looked Ty in his eyes.

"That's what I'm talking about." Marquis reminded Ty of himself when he was just stepping off the porch and green to the drug game. "I know you're not old enough to have a whip yet, so do you have a scooter or bike?" Marquis shook his head no. He hadn't thought that far into things, and he didn't have the money to go purchase one since he gave the hundred dollars that Ty gave him earlier in the week to his mother and had no friends he could borrow one from. He thought about going up to his mother's room to see if the money was still there but erased that idea from his head. "Don't worry, kid. Meet me back out here at one o'clock." Marquis agreed, and Ty hop-ped in his Benz and pulled off.

Marquis made his way inside and went into the kitchen and opened the fridge. He grabbed the pot full of beans and rice left over from the night before and sat it on the stove. His stomach began to growl as he set the front eye on high. "I was just about to do the same thing," Alexander stated, startling Marquis as he walked through the kitchen door. He made his way over to the kitchen cabinet and pulled out two plates and sat them on the table. They both sat down and waited patiently for the food to warm up.

"Yo, I just got finished talking to Ty," Marquis spoke, breaking the silence.

"Word, so what's the deal?"

"He told me to meet him out front at one o'clock." Alexander looked at the clock on the wall which read twelve noon.

"That's a hour from now." Mark looked up and agreed with a nervous look on his face.

"What if something goes wrong?" Alexander could see his brother was worried and having second thoughts. He knew he had to convince him before he decided to back out.

"Don't worry about what if something go wrong. We need to be making plans about what we gonna do once everything goes right. I'ma be right there by your side. Besides, as soon as we make the first run I know a place where we can cop a deuce deuce for a hundred dollars at."

Mark felt a little better hearing that news. He just hoped that everything went smoothly on their first run. He'd heard about people winding up missing after coming up short with the boss's money.

One o'clock came around quickly, and Marquis was in front of his building sitting on the front stoop waiting on Ty to pull up. Several fiends came walking up as well as in various vehicles looking for Ty. He couldn't wait to get in the game and be able to serve them. The thrill of the hustle excited him as he counted over a thousand dollars in fifteen minutes pass him by.

As fast as each one came, he would wave them

away just as fast. Five minutes later an old rusty

Chevy pickup with tinted windows rolled up.

"Ain't nuthin," Marquis told the driver with a

wave of his hand. When the driver didn't pull off

Marquis began to feel a little uneasy. As the

passenger's side window slowly came down

halfway, he heard a deep and scratchy male

voice.

"Ay, kiddo, you seen a nigga named Ty?"

Mark strained his eyes trying to get a good look

at the driver, but he couldn't. He wasn't about to

give any information out not knowing who was

asking. He could've been the police for all he

knew. He witnessed on several occasions that snitches get stitches, and he wasn't about to be labeled a snitch.

"Nah, my man, I don't know nobody by that name," Marquis responded with a lie.

"Very good," Ty replied as he rolled the window all the way down showing a mouth full of gold teeth. Marquis relaxed as he stood up and made his way over to the truck. "You passed the second test," Ty told him.

"Man, what are you doing in this old beat-up thing?" Marquis hit the side of the pickup then laughed.

"You can't always be flashy. Besides, there ain't no way possible I was gonna put your new bike in the back of my Benz." He got out of the truck, walked to the back of it, and then pulled the bike out of the back. Marquis's eyes grew as big as gold balls. There was the bike he'd been praying for the past two Christmases.

"That's a Diamondback," Marquis said out loud as Ty sat the bike in front of him. That was the Benz of all freestyle bikes.

"You like?" Marquis didn't say a word. The expression on his face said it all. "I couldn't have the newest member of my crew rolling on nothing but the best." That last statement alone made Marquis feel like a new person because he had never been a part of no one's crew, and for his first crew to be Ty's, he was really proud of himself.

"Thanks, Ty. I'll pay you back as soon as I make enough money."

"Don't worry about it, kid. Just think of it as an investment." Marquis didn't know exactly what he meant by that, but he was surely thankful. Now all he had to do was figure out how he was going to hide it from his mother. There was no way he could lie to her and say he found it like he told her he found the hundred-dollar bill he gave her earlier in the week. Ty saw the look on his face, but like always he had the perfect solution. "Whenever you finish making your runs for me you can put it in crackhead Tina's apartment over there." He pointed to the building across from where Marquis lived. Marquis thought he bought the bike for him to have, not just make runs for him on. Before he could get a word out Ty spoke again. "And whenever you want to just ride it, you can go and get it." A smile reappeared on Marquis's face as the thought of showing his new bike off to the kids in the neighborhood ran through his mind. Now all he had to do was get a chain and a lock because there was no way he was leaving it unattended in their neighborhood. "I'll have a run for you to make tomorrow around noon," Ty told him as he walked to the driver's side of the truck and hopped in.

"I'll be here waiting," Marquis assured him.

Before Ty could pull off, he called him to the passenger-side window.

"I almost forgot." Ty reached over and handed him a heavy-duty chain and a Masters lock. "Make sure you lock it up every time you get off of it." Marquis took them and promised to do just as he was told. "One more thing, we gotta do something about that name. From here on out have people to call you Mark, and your brother's new name will be Alex. Y'all's real names are too damn long." They both laughed. "Besides, you can't have motherfuckas calling you by your real name in these streets. That can get you fucked fast." Mark agreed, and as soon as Ty pulled off he locked his bike to the stair rail and raced into his apartment.

"Alexander, Alexander," Mark called out to his brother as he ran into their room.

"What's up?" Alexander asked as he hopped off the bed ready to go handle whoever had violated.

"Come outside; I got something I want to show you." Mark led the way and Alexander followed. When they made it outside, Alexander's mouth flew wide open.

"Is it yours?" he asked, figuring Mark had stolen it from someone.

"Yep," he proudly announced. "Ty got it for me." He walked over to it and unlocked it to prove it was his. When he got it unlocked he stood up and faced his brother. "Oh yeah, Ty said from here on out your name is Alex and I'm Mark. He said our names were too long, and besides we don't need everybody calling us by our real names in this game."

"I like dat," was all Alex said. Then he hopped on the bike and jetted down the block.

When he returned, he got off the bike, parked it, and went into his pocket and pulled out a piece of paper. "What's that?" Mark asked as he chained his bike back up.

"You remember that badass chick down the street named Torya?" Mark looked up toward the sky trying to put a face with the name Alex just called out.

"Yeah, why?" Mark asked, remembering the cute brown-skinned chick a few blocks down. A devilish grin spread across Alex's lips. "Stop lying," Mark said, not believing what his brother was implying. He gave him a look that let him know he was serious. "So what happened?"

"It happened like dis." Mark took a seat on the stoop while Alex stood in front of him ready to tell the story. Mark loved hearing Alex tell his stories, because he always talked with his body. "I went down a few blocks. When I got to the end, I turned the bike around to head back. On my way back, I saw a group of badass chicks on the sidewalk coming my way."

"So, what you do?" Mark asked as he slid to

the edge of the stoop to make sure he took in every detail.

"Well you know me," Alex said as he rubbed his chin like he was rubbing some hair on it. "I picked the front tire up in the air like this." Alex held his two arms out in front of him and balled up his fist like he was gripping a set of handlebars, then leaned back a little, and Mark caught himself doing the same. "I had it in the air so long, they couldn't believe it. When I brought it back down, Torya called me over, and that was it." Mark just shook his head at Alex, knowing how much of a show-off he could be at times. "Oh, there is one more thing."

"What's that?" Mark asked ready to hear

some more exciting news.

"I need to borrow your bike later on. I promised her I would take her riding later." They both laughed, and Mark agreed to let him take it for another spin. He figured he told Torya that it was his bike, but he didn't care because what was his was his brother's also. Mark kept his promise, and before the night was over he took his new bike over to Tina's apartment and then called it a night.

All through the night Mark tossed and turned until he finally dozed off to sleep. "Ay, Mark, wake up," Alex said as he stood over him rocking him back and forth. Mark lifted his eyes open and tried his best to focus on his brother's face.

"I'm up, I'm up." Mark wiped the cold from his eyes then stretched his arms wondering what Alex wanted.

"Yo, you know it is 12:16 right?" Mark still was confused. "Ty out front waiting on you. He told me to come and get you. He wouldn't tell me what he wanted though." Mark looked at the clock and jumped out of bed. Within seconds he had his pants and shoes on and was running out of their bedroom to the front door with Alex right behind him.

"Did he sound like he was mad?" Mark wanted to know while thinking of an excuse before he opened the door to walk outside.

"Chill, Bruh, I got you," Alex assured him.

"He was about fifteen minutes late when he pulled up, so I told him that you had just went into the house to use the bathroom." Mark smiled at his brother, glad that he had covered for him. He didn't want Ty to think he wasn't dependable or responsible on his first run. Alex stayed back while Mark went outside to handle his business.

When Mark opened the door he was blinded by the chromed-out 16-inch rims on Ty's Benz. "What up, kid? I'm running a little behind schedule today," Ty confessed. He gave Mark a pound and a short embrace. "I had kind of a long night, if you know what I mean." Ty Let out a light chuckle and waved his hand in the air, and out

of nowhere his do-boy Jun-Bug appeared out of

an abandoned apartment two buildings down.

When he approached he handed Ty a book bag

and then went back to where he was posted up

at. Ty and Mark both took a seat on the front

stoop while Ty peeped around checking out his

surroundings. After making sure everything was

good, he spoke. "I need for you to take this book

bag over to Yorel on Vance Street. You need to

have it there by one o'clock." That meant Mark

only had forty minutes to make the thirty-five-

minute ride to complete the run. "He gonna give

you an envelope. Don't open it," Ty stressed. He

looked into Mark's eyes to make sure he got the

point. "Once you get back I'll give you the five hundred we agreed upon." Mark wanted to ask why he couldn't get his off the top but decided against it. "Don't fuck this up, kid," Ty said with venom in his voice. Mark stood up as Ty headed to his Benz. When he was out of sight Mark headed over to Tina's apartment to get his bike. When he pulled it out, Jun-Bug was giving him the mean mug from across the street where he was still posted up. Mark figured he must've been jealous that it was him instead of Jun-Bug making the run. Mark jumped on his bike and paid him no mind. "I wonder where that punk ass Kessey at," he thought to himself. He looked down at his watch and realized he didn't have enough time to run in the apartment to get Alex if he wanted to be on time. "I'll let him roll the next time," Mark decided as he peddled off down the block to his destination.

He was nervous because the part of Vance Street he had to go to was right by Maplewood Avenue (a.k.a. the Mapes). That was one of Wilson's most ruthless neighborhoods. A lot of fights, stabbings, shootings, and murders happened on that end, and he knew since he didn't have a weapon at the time that he could easily be another statistic of the hood like many others in the past.

Once he reached Vance he felt a little more relaxed since no one was standing out on the block, but he wouldn't feel one hundred percent safe until he made it off with the envelope. He parked his bike up on Yorel's porch and walked up to the door. On the third knock he was let in by the doorman. "Last room on the right," he informed as he turned around and reapplied the chain lock, the two deadbolt locks, and a steel pole back up against the door.

When he walked through the room door where Yoreal was, he saw him lying across a dirty mattress with what appeared to be a crackhead's face buried in his lap. The room was kind of dark, so he couldn't make out who it was, but by the way Yorel was moaning and grinding, Mark knew it had to be some killer dome. Mark could feel himself getting hard from looking at the scene in front of him. When Yorel peeped up and saw Mark standing in the doorway, he quickly sat up and threw the covers over the crackhead trying to hide her identity. "I'll be out in a minute," Yorel yelled, signaling for Mark to step out so he could get dressed. Mark gave him a head nod and began to walk backward out the door, never taking his eyes off of them, trying to get one last peek to see if he could figure out who it was.

He closed the door behind him and waited in the hallway for about five minutes before Yorel finally came out zipping up his pants. "I'll be right back." He walked into the room beside the one he just came out of. When Yorel came back out, he could tell Mark was still a little hard from thinking about what he had seen earlier. "You want your dick sucked?" Yorel asked with a little smirk on his face. "It's the best on the market." Mark shook his head no, ready to get down to business. There was one rule he learned if he didn't learn anything else from watching movies, and that was never to mix business and pleasure together.

"You got the envelope?"

"And you know it!" Yorel replied as he pulled it out from his back pocket. Once he handed it to him he told Mark he needed for him to give Ty something else for him as well. Mark agreed, and Yorel went back into the room he just came out of. Mark was getting a little nervous and excited at the same time when the doorknob started to turn from the door where Yorel was getting some head when he first arrived. He was finally about to see the face of the crackhead with the super dome. When the door finally crept open and Super Dome stepped out, Mark's mouth damn near hit the floor. He stood there for a second hoping his eyes were playing tricks on him. He began to walk backward when he realized they weren't. He wanted to get out of there as fast as possible. Suddenly the room began to spin out of control. Yorel appeared with another envelope in his hand at the same time.

Mark's eyes shot from Yorel to Ty's main man Kessey, from Kessey back to Yorel. When Mark's eyes stopped on Kessey he knew he wasn't leaving out of there alive by the look in his eyes. "Damn," Mark thought to himself when he saw Kessey pull out the longest gun he had ever seen in his life. At least that's how scared he was. Any gun would've been big to him at that time. Mark was about to try his luck and bolt for the door, until he felt Yorel's huge arms yoke him up from the back.

"Yo, what we gonna do with him now?" Kessey asked Yorel, not wanting their secret to get out. He knew Ty would cut him off if he found out he went both ways, and even worse if it got out to his baby mama. She was known as the

Mouth of the South.

"I don't know. You think he'll tell anybody?"

They both looked at Mark and began to weigh

their options out. Before they could come up

with a conclusion, Mark yelled out, "I promise I

won't say a word to nobody."

Kessey's only reply was a sly grin, like he had

found the answer to their problem.

"I got an idea," he told Yorel as he slowly

walked over to him and whispered in his ear.

Yorel still had Mark in the yoke, and within

seconds, Mark felt Yorel's arm begin to tighten

up around his neck, and his feet lifted off the

ground. Mark fought as hard as he could to get

loose, but he was no match for the much stronger Yorel. Kessey swiftly snatched down Mark's pants and his holey boxers. Mark tried his best to fight. He swung and kicked wildly. To his surprise one of his kicks landed in Kessey's midsection.

"You little," Kessey shouted with a back-hand so hard to Mark's jaw that it knocked him out cold.

When Mark finally came to, he was lying across the same little dingy mattress he saw Kessey giving Yorel head on. Both his hands and feet were tied, and he was lying on his stomach.

"Well look who decided to join us, Yorel."

Mark's view became clearer as Kessey's and Yorel's bodies came into focus. They were both standing in front of him butt naked stroking themselves. Mark immediately tried to wiggle himself free. He knew his life would never be the same again, when he felt a stream of blood running down his legs from his asshole.

"My turn," Yorel greedily announce with a smile on his face as he positioned himself behind Mark ready to enter him.

"NOOOO," Mark screamed as he broke his hands and feet free from the rope.

"Mark, Mark, wake up, Bruh," Alex shouted as he tried to wake Mark from the nightmare he was having. Mark sat up and swung one last time into the air, almost connecting with a blow to the left side of Alex's face as he came to. He looked around and was relieved when he saw he was in his own room.

"Whew, it was only a bad dream," Mark said out loud.

"It must've been one hell of a dream, and you must've been getting your ass fucked up the way you were kicking and swinging." Alex started laughing. "You okay now?"

"Something like that, but I'm good now." Mark looked over at the clock and saw that it read 11:30 a.m. That meant he had thirty minutes to get himself together before Ty arrived. After Mark got dressed he went over to

Tina's and got his bike, so all he had to do was get the package from Ty, and him and Alex would be on their way to make the run.

Just like clockwork Ty arrived at 12:00 on the dot. Mark's heart dropped as the reflection of Ty's rims blinded him for a second, just like in his dream. "It was only a dream, it was only a dream," Mark repeated trying to convince himself.

"What you say?" Ty asked.

"Nothing," Mark replied erasing his thoughts. Ty went on and ran down the instruction to him then signaled Jun-Bug over. Everything began to feel like déjà vu as Mark's dream started to play itself out. He felt a little relieved when he found out he would be making the run to Cresent Gardens Apartments to J-Mudd instead of Vance Street.

J-Mudd was a well-known hustler in Wilson. He was a tall, slim, laidback cat with long dreads and a mouth full of gold teeth. He wasn't known for starting trouble, but the fact that he had a body under his belt got him plenty of respect.

When Ty bent the corner Alex immediately ran out of their apartment building ready to make their first run. "You ready?" Mark asked as he handed Alex the book bag.

"You know it," Alex excitedly responded as he put it on his back then jumped on the back pegs. He figured that would be the best way to travel just in case the police ran up on them or the jack boys tried to take their shit.

Ten minutes later they were pulling up in front of J-Mudd's apartment. Alex hopped off and handed Mark the book bag, so he could go handle business. Mark felt nervous knocking on the door. All that ran through his head was the dream he had the night before. "Come in," a male voice yelled from the other side. When Mark opened the door and made his way inside, he was amazed. In front of him was an all-white Italian sectional that covered the entire side of the living room, a huge picture of the famous Bob Marley smoking a blunt, and a 50-inch floor model television with a Nintendo hooked up to it. There were about a hundred games scattered over the floor to choose from. He looked at the television screen, and it looked like little midgets were playing football. "What you got for me?" J-Mudd asked pausing the game and breaking Mark out of his gaze. Mark didn't respond, just gave him the book bag once he walked over to him. J-Mudd inspected the contents inside and then headed to a room in the back. When he returned he handed Mark an envelope. He tucked it in his pocket and turned toward the door. "You wanna play Tecmo Bowl?" J-Mudd asked as he picked the controller back up and unpaused the game.

"Nah, maybe next time," Mark answered

over his shoulder never breaking his stride.

"How did it go?" Alex asked as he jumped back on the back pegs of the bike. Mark didn't answer. He had one thing and one thing only on his mind as they made their way back home.

~ ~ ~

"Yo, when we gonna go get that banger?"

"I thought you would never ask," Alex smiled. After following Alex's directions, Mark rolled up at the corner of Pender Street and Crowell Street to the garage door at Grant's Car Wash. As soon as Alex hopped off the back peg and Mark got off the bike and put it on its kickstand, they were greeted by one of the workers. "Yo, what y'all need?" he asked with a bucket and rag in hand like he was ready to wash Mark's bike.

"Man, crack is a powerful drug!" Mark thought to himself as Alex addressed the worker.

"Yo, have you seen Dez around here?" The worker's eyes lit up like a Christmas tree just thinking about how he was going to get a quick come-up off of the youngsters for the information he had for them. Right before he could run his game, the bell above the door of the Arab store across the street sounded, getting all of their attention. Then Dez walked out.

"Never mind." Alex smiled, grateful to be

able to avoid getting suckered out of a few

dollars for the worker's useless information.

"Dez," Alex called out, making his way

across the street in his direction.

"What-a-gwan, bredren?" Dez greeted as

he emptied out the guts of the White Owl Cigar

he held in his hand.

"Me and my brother need some fire," Alex

admitted. He turned and flagged Mark over, who

was still in front of the car wash getting harassed

by the worker.

"What y'all need?" Dez questioned as

Mark pushed his bike to where they stood.

"I got that Skunk, Mid, Dro, Purp,

Snoodie..." Dez ran down the list of weed he

had on him, pulling several ziplock bags out. Alex laughed.

"Not that kind of fire. A banger. A burner. Heat. Toast."

"Ohhh." Dez grinned. "Follow me to my car over here!" Dez turned on his heels and headed to the opposite side of the building to the dirt parking lot where his Crown Vic sat. After signaling for Mark to come along, Alex followed Dez. Once they were all at the trunk of Dez's car, he popped the trunk. "So how much y'all trying to spend?" Mark and Alex looked from one to the other. Neither one of them knew the price of a burner, but Mark didn't want to get burnt on the price, so he came up with the first number that came to his head.

"We got fifty dollars," he replied. He pulled a hundred-dollar bill out of the envelope J-Mudd gave to him for Ty. He secretly prayed that Ty wouldn't be mad with him for taking the fifty dollars out, but he needed the protection.

"Better safe than sorry," Mark reasoned and then handed it over to Dez.

"I don't got nothing for fifty, but that hundred will do." Dez slammed the trunk of his car down and then reached in the small of his back and retrieved a small, taped-up .22 revolver.

"Let me get that." Mark's heart dropped to the pit of his stomach. He couldn't believe that he was about to get robbed on his first day on the job for Ty. Alex's mind, on the other hand, was on taking the chance of rushing Dez and taking the gun out of his hand, but he realized that would not have been a smart idea since he would have had to reach around Mark to do it. When Mark handed Dez the entire envelope, Dex laughed.

"What's so funny?" Mark asked confused. Dez opened the envelope, took a hundred dollar bill out, and then handed it back to Mark.

"Bredren, selling drugs and guns is my job. I don't steal or rob," Dez continued, laughing. Mark let out a sigh of relief because he had no idea of how he was going to explain to Ty how he had gotten robbed of the envelope. After they shared a couple more laughs, they parted ways.

~ ~ ~

The first thing Mark saw when he turned his bike

onto his block was Ty chatting on his cell phone

outside of his Benz.

"I'll take the bike to Tina's house," Alex offered

when he hopped off of the bike's back pegs.

"Let me handle something right quick and I'll hit

you back when I'm on my way," Ty told the caller

on the other end. Mark looked as Ty frowned his

face up. "A condom for what?" he huffed and

then disconnected the call. When he looked at

Mark, all he could do was smile because he

reminded Ty of himself when he was that age:

young, hungry, and determined. "Get in." Mark

climbed into the passenger's seat as Ty walked around the front of the car and got in. After starting the engine, turning the A/C on blast, and turning down the radio, Ty directed his attention to his new protégé. "So how did things go on your first run?" Ty asked. Mark was so amazed by the car's electronics, Ty had to ask him again before he could get a response.

"Everything went good," he finally answered, still looking at the dashboard. Mark then went into his pocket and pulled out the envelope that J-Mudd had given him. Without inspecting the contents, Ty pulled out five one-hundred-dollar bills and handed them to Mark. "What's this for?" Ty asked when Mark handed him a hundred dollars back. Ty thought that he was trying to repay him for the hundred that he gave him earlier in the week.

"I know you told me not to go into the envelope, but I bought a burner for protection for me and my brother," Mark admitted. He proudly showed Ty the old taped-up .22 revolver he had purchased from Dez. Ty concealed his laughter by bobbing his head up and down in approval. Even though Ty laughed on the inside, he was very proud of the decision Mark had made. Unlike Mark, Ty and many other starting-out hustlers decided to blow their first real money on girls, jewelry, clothes, or shoes.

"Y'all are going to be a force to be reckoned

with," Ty thought after he dismissed Mark from his car and watched him take his apartment steps two at a time to the front door. Instead of putting the hundred-dollar bill back in the envelope, Ty called Mark back to the car. When he approached, Ty handed the bill out the window. "Give this to Alex for me." Mark agreed and then listened to Ty run down the runs he had for them the following day. When he was done, they dapped each other up. Once Mark entered the apartment, Ty went into his pocket, took out a bottle of yellow pills, and popped one in his mouth. After chasing it down, Ty took out his cell and called one of his jump-offs to go release some built-up stress.

4

SHIT DONE CHANGED
LATER THAT NIGHT...

After dinner Mark and Alex headed to their

room at full speed. "Let me see it again," Alex

asked as he closed the door behind them. They

both rushed to the foot of their bed, and Mark

bent over and pulled an old Cuga shoe box from

under it. and removed the old taped-up .22

revolver pistol from it. They looked at it in

amazement. They had both seen a gun before,

but never up close and personal. This was the

first time Mark ever held one in his hands

besides when he first purchased it. He loved the feel of the cold steel in his hands. He gripped it with both hands like he had his enemy in his scope and acted like he was pulling the trigger. "BANG," he said out loud as his sister, Nicole, entered the room without knocking. She took a deep breath, and her mouth was stuck in the shape of the letter O. Before a sound could escape her mouth or before she could turn around and run back out, Alex ran over to her and put his hands over her mouth and then quickly shut the door behind her before she could turn around and run back out.

"I'm so sorry, Nicole," Mark apologized once Alex sat her down at the edge of the bed. She sat there trembling for a while before she finally was able to speak.

"What are you doing with that?" she asked as she pointed to the gun he still had in his hand. All she could think about was the fight her brothers had at the arcade with Big Curt, Quick, and Nitty on the last day of school. She didn't want anyone to get hurt behind her, and most of all she didn't want her brothers going to jail. Mark tried his best to calm her down.

"It's for protection, that's all," was all he said, and by the look he had on his face she knew asking anything else about it was a waste of time, so she let it go. There was no way he was going to tell her what he and Alex had gotten into. He knew that it would eventually come out, but for now, the less she knew the better things were. After promising she wouldn't tell their mother, they gave her ten dollars apiece hush money and then sent her on her way.

A week passed, and they made runs for Ty every day. Sometimes they would even make two or three runs in a single day. Their pockets were getting fatter and fatter, and the Williams Brothers name started to become known by the streets.

After each run they made they would buy an outfit and a pair of shoes to go with it. The following week they bought chains with matching bracelets to set it off. By the end of the summer they were flier than any kid in their neighborhood. Carolyn started noticing her children's appearances, so she would ask questions concerning their gear. They even looked out for Nicole for keeping her promise. They convinced their mother that they had jobs at the local grocery store making deliveries, which they felt wasn't a complete lie since they were making deliveries. At the end of each week the brothers would give Carolyn a hundred dollars apiece just as they planned. At that point they sat Nicole down and had a talk with her and broke everything down to her. Even though she didn't agree with what they were doing, she had her brothers' backs. Through her young years she'd seen the effect drugs and the game could have on people. She wanted to speak her piece but knew when her brothers' minds were made up, they were made up.

When school started back Nicole and Alex stayed at the middle school they attended the previous year, but this year was much different for the two siblings. Their entire appearance had changed. Instead of sharing three pairs of pants with his brother, now Alex had a collection of clothes to choose from, such as Gap, Nautica, Tommy Hilfiger, Girbaud, and Polo. His shoe game was crazy. Each day he would wear the latest pair of Jordans, Bo Jacksons, Patrick Ewings, or Penny Hardaways. Last year girls use to walk right by him, but now it was like they broke their necks to be noticed by him. He felt like he was on a whole nother level now. After the word got out that him and Mark were running packages for Ty, kids at his school admired him, mostly the girls, and the guys now respected him. The ones that didn't got taught firsthand and quickly made examples of. It was then they learned Alex could handle his with or without his older brother. Having Torya by his side made a big difference as well since she was the prettiest chick at their school now.

Nicole, although now dressed much flier than most of the girls at her school, was still the same ole shy person as before. Her two brothers spoiled her rotten and treated her like a true queen. Needless to say, they kept an even closer eye on her now. A lot of guys wanted to try to get with her but were afraid because they all knew of her brothers' reputation of beating guys down for even looking at her the wrong way. She kind of liked the attention she was receiving but didn't let it go to her head and kept her mind on her education. She knew her body had developed even more over the summer and that guys would say anything to get what boys wanted from a girl. She wasn't into boys though. She knew if she wanted anything all she had to do was let one of her brothers know and it was hers.

Mark walked into Fike High School with a new look as well. He no longer looked down when he walked past his peers. He glided through the halls with his head held high and full of confidence. His ego shot sky high every time he would walk past a group of so-called cool kids and the first thing he heard was "Who's the new guy?" It shocked him because most of them were the same ole kids that used to giggle at him when he walked by the year before.

"Look how time and money changes things," he thought to himself as he kept on walking. The crazy thing about it all was that some even knew his name. Some of the females were all-out bold with theirs and would stop him and compliment him on his gear and rub his chain. He figured they were trying to see if it was thin or how heavy it was. He felt like he was on top of the world for the first time in his life.

On his way to his homeroom class his heart suddenly skipped a beat. He stood frozen in one spot as she walked in his direction with the most beautiful smile on her face. "Long time no see, stranger," Tosha said as she stopped in front of him. This was the first time he had seen her since the scene at the arcade a few months ago, even though he thought about her every day after that. A smile appeared on his face as he took in her beauty. She noticed the look in his eyes and could see that he wasn't the same little nerdy and shy guy from last school year, and by the look of his gear and jewelry she knew he had definitely stepped his game up. "So how was your summer?" When he responded she knew his confidence was up and now through the roof as well.

"It was cool. I can see the summer was good to you. Look at you," he complimented gesturing to her outfit. He then took a step backward and admired the way her Christian Dior sweat suit hugged each and every one of her many curves. He could tell his compliment really shocked her because she was the one blushing now. She didn't know it, but every day since he saw her at the arcade, he would go there hoping to see her, but he never did. Her dimples seemed to be even deeper as she stood in front of him smiling.

"I can see it was even better to you," she shot back trying to reverse the scene and take control of the situation. She reached over and fixed his collar as the bell rung for everyone to go to their homeroom classes to get their schedule for the year.

"Let me walk you to your class?" he asked as he took her books from her arms before she could answer him. She smiled and then turned around to lead the way. Girls screwed their faces up knowing their chances of being chosen by him were slim to none now since the couple walked together like no one else was in the hall with them. To both of their surprise, they had the same homeroom class. They made their way to the back where there were two empty seats beside each other.

After they got their schedule for the first semester, they realized that they shared two more classes together. Mark was glad because now he would not have to try to be wherever she was just to see her. By the end of the day they exchanged numbers with promises to call each other later.

The school year seemed to fly by, and Mark and Alex grew. Not just in height, but in juice and cash flow as well. Their names became the topic of every hoodrat and up-and-coming hustler that wanted to be with the Williams Brothers. Little did they know they were also quickly making as many enemies in the process.

"Yo, you remember last year when that chick and her two brothers walked through here, and we almost had to put hands on them two niggas?" Big Kev asked D.J. D.J. inhaled the blunt smoke as he thought back to the time that Big Kev was referring to.

"Oh yeah. You talking about shorty with the phat ass that got the two brothers?" he recalled. "The one that Rodney got the eye on?"

"Yeah, that's her," Kev snapped. Then he snatched the dangling blunt from between D.J.'s lips. "You know them two niggas done some how come up, don't you?" he asked as he let out a huge cloud of smoke.

"Word. That's wassup," D.J. smiled thinking back to the day he came up in the game.

"Nah. That ain't wasup," Big Kev claimed between coughs. "I'm trying to see them two niggas!" Big Kev inhaled again then blew the smoke out in large circles. He stared off into space, thinking of a way to get at Mark and Alex. His thoughts got interrupted by the sound of Rodney's voice.

"What y'all two niggas out here plotting on?" he asked his Little Homies. D.J. was about to answer until Big Kev elbowed him in his side to

103

silence him.

"Nothing, big homie," Big Kev answered slyly.

He knew if he revealed his true intentions,

Rodney would discipline him for sure.

"Yeah, whatever." Rodney waved him off then

took the blunt out of his hand. "I'm about to step

off for a few hours. Y'all niggas hold the fort

down," Rodney ordered. Then he walked off the

porch and headed to his Cadillac. As soon as

Rodney bent the corner, Big Kev spoke his

mind.

"Yo, man, why your cousin on those two lil

niggas' sister anyway?"

D.J. shrugged his shoulders and said, "I don't

even know, homie, but if she knew any better,

she would stay as far away from that bi-polar-ass nigga as possible." D.J.'s mind drifted back to a couple of summers ago when Rodney caught a rape charge. If it wasn't for the girl's mother being a regular customer of their trap house, and the fact that Rodney gave her a half an ounce of crack, the charges would have never been dropped. D.J. was brought back to the present by the sound of Big Kev's voice.

"Those nigga's are mine," he promised. D.J. looked at Big Kev from out of the corner of his eyes then shook his head.

"Hatin'-ass nigga," he thought to himself. Then he hit the blunt one more time before passing it to Big Kev.

5

THE ORANGE CRUSH

Mark and Alex were waiting outside sitting on the front stoop of their apartment building watching all the fly honeys walk by dressed in next to nothing, vying for their attention. The two brothers weren't interested in them though. All they had on their minds was making money. "We done came a long ways in a year's time," Alex told his brother with a big grin on his face while basking in all the attention he was now receiving.

"Yeah we have, haven't we?" Mark agreed thinking back to when the girls paid them no attention at all when they wore rags for clothes. Now they had all the latest and flashiest gear out. They often changed clothes twice a day without wearing the same thing twice in a month. "I was thinking about copping a whip in the next week or two."

"Word, what kind?" Alex asked as he covered his mouth with a closed fist. He was hyped off the idea of riding shotgun.

"I saw dis badass black Type-2 Acura Legend with chrome rims." Alex slowly bobbed his head up and down in approval. Before Alex could say something else, they heard a loud stereo system coming from a car turning on their block. They both looked up and saw Ty's Benz slowly pulling up to the curb in front of them. Ty hopped out, and the two brothers stood up and met him on the sidewalk where they showed each other love.

"I'm really impressed with how y'all been handling business over the past year," Ty announced proudly as he looked at his protégés. "Not even once has my money come up short with you two." Mark and Alex did whatever they had to do to make sure Ty's money was always on point, and sometimes when people came up short or tried to beat Ty out of his product, for a few more hundred they would straighten the person out. "I got a surprise for y'all tonight." He looked at the excitement in their eyes and smiled before he continued. "I'll fill y'all in more once y'all return from y'all's last run. I only got two runs for y'all today. Is that cool?" They shook their head up and down. They really didn't care how many runs they had for the day. All that was on their minds was the surprise that awaited them when they were finished. They both hoped it was money, remembering the $2,000 apiece bonus they got the last time Ty had a surprise for them. Ty gave them their instructions, and as usual Jun-Bug appeared from the abandoned apartment with the package.

The two runs went smoothly, and Mark and Alex were finished before the sun went down. As soon as they turned the corner to their block they saw Ty out in front of their apartment building along with his two flunkies, Kessey and Jun-Bug. "Did everything go as expected?" Ty asked when Mark and Alex got off the bike.

"Have we ever let you down?" Mark asked with a smile on his face, handing him the envelope.

"I wish all my help was like y'all two," Ty stated, then looked at Kessey and Jun-Bug. He slid the envelope into his pocket knowing there was no need to count it behind him. "Y'all niggas need to take notes from Mark and Alex." Kessey and Jun-Bug just mean-mugged the two brothers. They knew not to get out of line. They remembered firsthand what it felt like to get on Ty's bad side. "Okay now, back to business." Ty rubbed his hands together like he was warming them up over a warm fireplace. The brothers broke their staring contest with the flunkies and waited patiently for Ty to go on. "I want y'all two to get dressed in the fliest shit y'all got and meet me back out here at eleven tonight. I'ma let y'all roll with me tonight and show y'all how a real boss gets down, everything on me." Kessey and Jun-Bug both screwed their faces up at Mark and Alex even more after they heard what Ty had said. In their entire three years of hustling for Ty he never once offered them to go out with him. The brothers paid no attention to the looks they received and agreed to be ready at that time. After Ty broke them off with two grand apiece, he jumped in his Benz with Kessey and Jun-Bug right behind him.

"Yo, how I look, Bruh?" Alex asked as he did a three sixty in the middle of the floor. He wore a pair of Nautica jeans and a blue-and-red Nautica button up. He topped it off with a pair of blue Nautica sneakers with a big sailboat on the side of them in red. His Gucci link bracelet matched his Gucci link chain which carried a diamond incrusted Uzi charm at the end of it. Mark smiled at how his brother had stepped up his game from the T-shirt or black hoodie look

he loved so much.

"You almost look as good as me," Mark

joked as he popped his collar. He took a look at

himself in the full-length mirror on the back of

their door. With a flick of his wrist he brushed off

his shoulders and then looked down at his Polo

jeans making sure they didn't sag too far below

his waist. He turned around and looked at the

Polo jockey riding the horse that covered up the

entire back of his shirt. "Ay, yo, me and the nigga

riding on the horse got on the same kind of

shoes." Mark laughed as he looked down at his

Polo boots. Alex shook his head and laughed at

how conceited his brother was acting. He was

113

proud of how his older brother had come up and didn't leave him out like he had seen so many other brothers do in the past. Mark ran his fingers over his 40-inch Cuban link chain and then put on the matching bracelet. Alex tried to talk him into buying an iced-out Jesus piece charm, but Mark simply told him, "The chain speaks for itself," and that was that.

"Whatever, nigga, don't hate." They both laughed and then put on a dab of cologne. After giving themselves a once over, they went out front and waited on Ty.

Just like clockwork, Ty pulled up at eleven o'clock in a new Benz. He stepped out and smiled as Mark and Alex both stood up, stepped off the stoop, and stared in amazement. "Dammnnn," they shouted. Then they walked up and stared at Ty's new S420 with the AMG kit around it.

"You like?" Ty asked as he walked up beside them and looked at the 18-inch AMG rims. He bought it after he left them earlier. "Watch this." Ty went into his pocket and pulled out a remote and hit a button. The engine came to life, and all four windows rolled halfway down.

"I got front seat," Mark claimed as he ran to the passenger side and hopped in. Alex got in the back seat behind his brother as Ty went to the driver's side.

As soon as they turned the corner to the

club, they could see cars lined up on both sides of the street from light to light. "I know all these people are not going in the club," Mark said as Ty pulled his car directly in front of the Orange Crush. When they stepped out of the Benz, all eyes were on them. "Look at that big-body Benz," they heard a few chicks whisper over the rest of the gossip. Instead of walking around to the side of the club to get in line, Ty walked straight to the front and approached the bouncer. He gave the bouncer some dap and a quick embrace and then whispered a few words in his ear all at the same time. To the untrained eye it was impossible to see Ty slide him a few bills. When they broke the embrace, the bouncer looked up and motioned for Mark and Alex to go in.

When they got inside it was as if they had stepped into another world. The club was live and filled to capacity. There were ladies in all shapes, forms, colors, and sizes choosing and waiting to be chosen. Ty walked straight to the grill area and ordered a plate of chicken wings, fish, and fries with three large teas. "We gonna need this," Ty warned with a devilish grin. He learned early in the game what it felt like to drink on an empty stomach. After their order came up, they took a seat at a booth, and within five minutes everything was gone. "Follow me," Ty said as he made his way to the bar on the opposite side of the club. The more they walked, the more chicks came in view. Mark and Alex had never seen so many girls in one place at one time looking like supermodels. "Let me get a bottle of Dom P and whatever my friends want." They both smiled hearing Ty referred to them as his friends instead of his workers. They had never been to a club before, so they didn't know what to order. As a matter of fact, they had never even taken a drink of alcohol before. They quickly thought of a drink they heard rappers always bragging about and went with that.

"I'll have a bottle of Moet please," Alex asked.

"And I'll have a bottle of Cris," Mark told the

bartender as if he always ordered that bottle. Ty pulled out a wad of money and paid for their drink as if he just paid for three bottles of spring water. He then excused himself to the restroom.

"Look at you two niggas!" Mark and Alex heard a familiar voice call out from behind them. When they turned around, they were greeted by their first cousin on their father's side of the family.

"Yo, what up, cousin?" Alex said. He stood up and showed him some love. Romeo was the true live wire of the family. He took his calling to the streets a few years before Mark and Alex. He gained his respect and was known as a knock-out artist as well as a vicious gunslinger.

It was rumored that he had a couple of bodies in the last year alone.

They chopped it up for a couple of minutes until a sexy, thick chick joined his side and whispered something in Romeo's ear. "Well, cousins, I'll get up with y'all later." After exchanging numbers, Romeo parted ways.

~ ~ ~

Thirty minutes later they were side by side sipping on their bottles, It was easy to see that they were the main attraction of the club, and they knew it. Mark and Alex were feeling the buzz from their half-empty bottles of champagne as chicks flaunted by them half naked. Being that Mark and Alex never got attention like that before, they wanted to get with each and every

one of them. Ty laughed at his protégés and

stopped them each time they would look at him

for his approval. They knew if he shook his head

no, that the chick was no good or that he had

already fucked her before.

Mark and Alex began to grow tired of Ty

rejecting all the females that tried to dance with

them and began to think he was too picky or just

downright hating. Mark felt a light tap on his

shoulder and heard a soft female voice from

behind. "Can I have a dance, cutie?" she asked

as she wrapped her arms around his waist.

When he turned around he couldn't believe his

eyes. He had to take a double take to make sure

the champagne wasn't playing tricks with his eyes. Tosha was standing there directly in front of him looking better than ever in a tight-fitting Guess dress. He looked over at Ty, and he nodded his head in approval. It really didn't matter what Ty said, he was going to dance with her regardless. The only problem he had now was that he didn't really know how to dance.

"I don't know how to dance," he confessed to her.

"That's cool. All you have to do is just stand there and look cute like you been doing, and I'll handle the rest." She gave him a seductive look and guided him onto the dance floor. Just as she was about to drop it low on him, the D.J.

changed it up and put on "Let's Chill" by Guy.

She turned around with her back facing him then

reached her arms behind his neck and began

winding her backside against his crotch. He ran

his hands up and down her side before placing

them onto her hips. He was so much in a zone

from her body movement, he felt like they were

one. She slowly turned around, wrapped her

arms around his shoulders, and rested her head

on his chest. Mark was disappointed when the

D.J. changed the mood and put on some faster

music. When Mark looked to each side of him,

to his surprise Alex and Ty had two chicks bent

over touching the floor while they had their

bottles glued to their lips with one hand and

slapping their asses with the other. Mark laughed, knowing his brother was fucked up. Tosha grabbed Mark's hand and pulled him off the dance floor to a dimly lit booth in the back. "I didn't know you be coming here."

"I usually don't, but Ty brought us out here with him," Mark admitted. "This is our first time."

"Mine too," Tosha replied honestly. She took the bottle of Cris off the table and took a sip. "Ewww," she said as she quickly sat it back down. "I don't see what they like about that drink."

"Me either." They both burst into laughter. They made small talk, and before they knew it the lights came on and the D.J announced that it was time for everyone to make their exit. Mark could tell that she wasn't ready for their night to end, and neither was he.

"Well I guess this is it," she told him with a weak smile.

"I guess so." They both stood up from the booth and locked eyes.

"Yo, we about to bounce to Denny's," Alex said as he walked up breaking their awkward moment of silence. "Come on, y'all." After seeing they both didn't move, he knew he had to talk some more. "Tosha, you better hurry up if you gonna catch up with your girls." She still didn't budge. "That's if you gonna join us for breakfast." That last statement got her attention.

She looked at Mark to see if it was cool with him. The smile on his face said it all, and Tosha knew it. "We'll be waiting in the car," Alex said before he walked off to give them a little privacy. When Tosha was about to walk away, Mark grabbed her hand. When she turned back around, he took off his chain and placed it around her neck. He had to overlap it twice, making it look like she had on two Cuban link chains. She couldn't believe her eyes as she ran her hand over it. She craned her neck up and gave him a little peck on his lips.

"I'll see you at Denny's," she shouted over her shoulder as she walked out of the club. She knew Mark would be watching her, so she decided to put a little extra sway in her walk.

After pushing and shoving his way through the groupies and haters, he finally made it out front just to find out there were even more surrounding Ty's Benz. "Back seat," Alex pointed once Mark reached the passenger door. Mark was too high on cloud nine to argue with him, so he just opened the back door and climbed in the back. All he had on his mind was eating breakfast with his future wife.

On the ride to Denny's they all laughed and talked about the fun they had that night and made arrangements to do it again soon in the near future. Ty glanced in the rearview mirror at his protégé and couldn't do anything but smile as he looked into his eyes. He knew that look all too well. He wanted to say something, but he didn't. He knew that was a road every man would travel and experience on their own no matter what a person told him about it. He just hoped love didn't blind him. When he took his eyes off him, he had to take another look when he noticed Mark's chain was no longer around his neck. "Yo, kid, where da fuck your chain?" Mark touched his neck, and Ty noticed his facial expression change, not out of worry, but happiness. Ty was about to turn around and head back to the club to look for it.

"My shorty got it on," Mark replied in a slurred voice.

"Awww, man, how you gonna let the broad whip you without even getting the pussy first?" Alex yelled out, making Ty burst into laughter.

"Fuck y'all niggas," Mark joked then joined in. When they walked in the place, they spotted the girls sitting in a booth in the back. They all staggered over as every eye in the restaurant rested on them. Most of the looks came from the chicks that were checking them out, and the rest came from the haters they were with. Either way they didn't worry about them because they had the prettiest chicks in the building. Also, Ty was strapped.

Once the waitress left with their orders, they sat around getting to know one another a little better. Ty was the main attraction now due to the fact that he told a lot of interesting stories and kept everyone wanting to hear more.

After eating, Ty paid for everyone's food and left a hefty tip while the rest of them went outside. In the parking lot, Mark and Tosha stood off to the side and said their good-nights, followed by a long and passionate tongue kiss. Not to mention a few rubs here and there.

Mark watched Tosha and her friends pull out of the parking lot and then made his way to Ty's car. When he got in, all eyes were on him. "What?" Mark asked with a new glow on his face. Ty and Alex just turned back around to the front shaking their heads knowing Mark was gone over Tosha.

They got on Highway 264 and headed back to the hood. The entire way back all Mark could think about was Tosha and how soft her lips felt. He vowed not to wash his lips again. "I knew she would be mine," Mark said to himself while thinking how his plan was all coming together.

6

THE LEGEND

The following week Mark and Alex were on their grind like never before. They hustled from sun up to sun down every single day. Mark had stacked up so much, he confided in Ty about copping a new whip, and just as Ty promised every night after Mark completed all his runs, he would take him to the country and teach him how to drive. Not on the Benz, of course. It didn't matter to Mark one way or the other as long as he learned. He knew deep down inside that one day he would be styling like Ty, if not even better.

The weekend came when Mark was ready to cop his new whip. Ty picked him, and Alex up as promised, then explained to him that he was going to take him to where he got his car from in Raleigh on Capital Blvd. He said they had a lot of tricked-out foreign cars there. "Yo, I'm telling you that Arabia motherfucka will sell you the shirt off his mama's back if you got the money." They all burst out laughing, but that was music to Mark's ears because he hadn't tried for his license yet and he wasn't for sure whose name he was going to put it in.

Mark took the Type-2 Acura Legend for a

test drive with Alex right beside him. As soon as he hit the accelerator, he fell in love with it instantly. Everything about it stood out, from its triple black paint job to its black-on-black interior. Alex toyed with the six-disc cd changer and made a call from the mobile phone located in the armrest to a chick he had met at the mall the day before, but what really made Mark know that was the car for him was the rush he felt when he pressed the gas to the floor and the power stuck his back to the seat.

Mark pulled back into the dealership smiling from ear to ear. The lot owner had a huge grin on his face as well. He knew by the look Mark had on his face that he was going to buy it. Mark hopped out of the coupe with only one thing on his mind. "How much?" The Arabian's grin grew into a full-blown Kool-Aid smile hearing those words. At that time Alex went over to Ty's Benz and grabbed a book bag and then walked back toward the Arab, who immediately knew it contained the money.

"Right this way, my friend." The Arab extended his arm out and pointed in the direction of his office. Before they entered the small building, the Arab told one of the workers to clean and fill it up while they completed the paperwork.

Thirty minutes later after informing the dealer that he didn't have any license at the time plus an extra two grand, Mark was given the title and signed all the necessary papers. When they walked back out to his new car, Alex was already sitting in the front seat. By the time he got in and started the car Ty pulled up beside him and told him that he would follow until they got on the highway. Mark nodded his head in agreement as Alex turned up the radio. "Yo, that's my shit," Mark shouted out as he put more volume to it and began to sing the lyrics to Kool G. Raps hit single, "Road to Riches."

Once they got on Highway 264 headed back to Wilson, Alex picked up the mobile phone and dialed Ty's number. As soon as he answered Alex yelled into the phone, "You ain't trying to run it!" By that time Ty was riding beside them, so he looked over in their direction. Ty was about to say something, but before he could, Mark slammed his foot on the gas and was slowly pulling away from Ty. Ty just shook his head, hung up his cell, and then let the V* do all the talking. Mark looked up in his rearview and saw Ty coming up on him fast. He couldn't believe Ty was gaining on him. He looked at his speed odometer, and it read 120 MPH and climbing. Ty pulled up beside them like it was no big deal and put up his pointer finger and began to shake it from side to side letting them know that they didn't stand a chance.

"Oh shit," Alex yelled. Then he pointed up at

the bridge bypass. When Ty and Mark looked up they saw a state trooper jump inside of his patrol car and hit his lights. Ty and Mark made eye contact with each other. Ty smiled at him and threw up the peace sign and then mashed his gas pedal to the floor. Within a minute flat his tail-lights disappeared in the distance.

"Yo, that was close," Mark admitted when they made it back to the city limits. He glanced in his rearview mirror to make sure that the state trooper wasn't still behind them.

"For real," Alex agreed while turning down the radio. "Where we headed, Bruh?" he asked once Mark made a right on Vance St. and passed Barton College.

"Just chill for a minute." Mark picked up his mobile phone, dialed a few numbers, and waited for the caller to answer. "May I speak to Tosha?"

"Whipped-ass nigga," Alex joked as he shook his head from side to side. Before Mark had a chance to speak on his brother's comment, Tosha spoke into the receiver.

"Come outside. I'm in front of your house." Just when she was about to ask him how he got over to her house, he hung up, leaving her holding the phone in her hand. "You look beautiful," hc greeted when he stepped out of his car and met her halfway, making her blush.

"Whose car is this?" she asked after their short hug.

"You like?" he asked as he took a step back to give her a clear view of his new car.

"I love it." Tosha opened the driver door and sat down in the driver seat.

"Hey, Alex."

"What's up, sis?" Tosha smiled as she gripped the steering wheel and envisioned herself driving down the highway. She caught Mark and Alex grinning from ear to ear at how she got caught up in the moment.

"I just wanted to stop by and surprise you," Mark announced when Tosha got out of the car and shut the door behind her.

"Thank you. It's always a nice surprise seeing you." Now it was Mark's turn to blush.

Just when he was about to comment, Tosha's mother came to the door to let her know it was time for her to eat. "I'll call you later." Before she went back into the house, she gave him a hug and a peck on the lips. Mark watched the door close behind her before he hopped in his car and pulled off. Needless to say, Alex joked on his lovesick brother all the way back to the hood

As soon as Mark turned the corner to their block, the first person they saw was Ty. He was sitting on the hood of his car sipping on a bottle of Remy with a bottle of Coke beside him. "What took y'all niggas so long?" Ty asked once they got out of the car. "I been waiting on y'all for about an hour." He took another swallow and

141

waited for a response.

"You know I had to go and show my girl our new car," Mark smiled and then rubbed his hand through the goatee that was starting to form under his chin. "Then we rode through all the hoods to show how we rolling on this side of town." Ty looked at the brothers dap each other up. He had to admit that he was proud of how they had come up under his wing. They'd proven to really be worthy of being put down with his crew. He just wished he could say the same about his other two crew members.

"Yo, whatever happened to that state trooper anyway?" Ty asked out of the blue. "I thought I was going to have to come bail y'all guys out or something." He laughed and finished off his bottle.

"After the first mile I didn't see his lights flashing in my rearview anymore, so I couldn't tell you what happened to him. Once I got up to a buck fifty, it was a wrap." Mark laughed as he tapped the hood of his car. After they joked a little more and Ty ran down the plans for tomorrow's runs, they parted ways, Ty going to beat some young girl back out that he met earlier that week and Mark and Alex going into the apartment to do as they did every night before they went to sleep, calling Tosha and Torya.

7

KILLER INSTINCT

Ever since Mark got his car, he and Tosha had become a lot closer than before. As a matter of fact, it was like they were inseparable now. Where you saw one, you were bound to see the other, and today was no exception.

Mark offered to pick Tosha up from her house, but she declined and told him that she was riding with one of her girlfriends and would meet him at the arcade. After he agreed, he promised to be on time after he made his last delivery. They ended their call, and Mark slapped Alex's leg to wake him up. "What, man?" he asked, still half sleep.

"Come on. Get up. It's about that time." Alex sat up, stretched his arms, and yawned.

"Who were you just talking to?" Alex wanted to know.

"Why?"

Alex was sure Mark was in love with Tosha even though he'd always play the subject to the left by saying they were good friends. Alex then asked the question Mark had also been avoiding. "Yo, Bro, when you gonna tell her what you really do for money?" He looked at Alex while wondering the same thing himself. "You know she ain't gonna keep going for that lame delivery-boy shit with you constantly spending cheddar on her," Alex said as he picked a pillow up from their bed and hit Mark in the head with it, snapping him out of his thoughts of how long his plan would last.

"I'll tell her when I feel the time is right," he replied while picking the pillow up off the floor and throwing it back at Alex, hitting him in the face. They had a pillow fight that ended with them wrestling for a few minutes until Alex was out of breath.

"You lucky we weren't throwing punches," Alex warned, knowing Mark wouldn't have won going blow for blow.

"Yeah, yeah, yeah," Mark responded while pulling Alex off the floor. He knew Alex was telling the truth because out of all the fights he had been in no one had ever hit him as hard as his brother. After Alex was to his feet, he shot a quick two piece in the air in Mark's direction, a left toward his jaw then a quick right jab to the body. "Aight, nigga," Mark warned as he felt the wind come from his blows. They both laughed as Alex headed for the shower and Mark got dressed.

When Ty arrived, they greeted each other as usual, and then Jun-Bug appeared from the abandoned apartment. "Is everything aight?" Mark asked after noticing Ty seemed a little more distant than normal.

"Yeah, I'm good, kid, just got some things on my mind." He saw Mark's expression on his face change. "It's nothing for you to worry about though," Ty assured him. Mark shook his head up and down and figured if Ty wanted to tell him more about it, he would, so until then he'd let it go. Ty gave them the instructions they needed for the run and then jumped back in his Benz and sped off as if he was in a hurry.

Today they only had to drop off one package on Vick Street to a guy name Los.

Los was a young hustler from the east side of Wilson. Even though he was young in age, he still held his own in the game. He drove big-boy bikes and cars, made big-boy money, and fucked big-boy bitches, which entitled him to make big-boy moves, and that was the reason he gained big-boy respect.

When they pulled up to his spot, Alex handed Mark the package and followed him up on the porch were Los's in man B.G. was sitting with three other guys playing spades. "That ass sought," B.G. screamed as he slammed the ace of spades down on the tabletop cutting his opponent's queen of diamonds.

"Nigga, why the fuck you trying to skate with the queen of diamonds?" B.G.'s opponent asked his partner. "Wit yo stupid ass," he continued while reaching in his pocket and pulling out two one-hundred-dollar bills to pay for his loss. B.G. gladly accepted his winnings and watched him walk off the porch and down the steps.

"Yo, what up, B.G.?" Alex asked as he showed his homey some love.

"Ain't shit, just breakin' these niggas, you know what I mean?" B.G. asked as he pointed to the two guys he just beat in spades turning the corner. They both laughed because Alex saw B.G. pull a card out of a book that was already played before. "What up, Mark? Los is in there waitin' on you." Mark nodded his head and made his way into the spot while Alex stayed on the porch and chopped it up with B.G.

and his homie.

"What's good with you, playboy?" Los asked as he stood up and gave Mark some dap.

"Same ole shit, just a different day," Mark responded as he returned the love and handed over the book bag. He didn't even check it just as Mark didn't check the envelope once Los handed it to him. They talked for a minute or two before Mark made his exit.

Later on, that night Ty called Mark to make sure he was home so he could come by to collect his money. Before ending the call, he let Mark know that he needed to have a talk with him as well.

When Ty arrived, Mark noticed he had the

same look on his face from earlier. "So, what's good, big homie?" Mark asked after handing Ty the envelope. Ty tucked the money away and then looked into Mark's eyes. Mark had no idea what Ty wanted to talk to him about, but what came out of his mouth was unbelievable.

"The last few packages I had you to drop off for me been coming short when I know they shouldn't of been because I put a couple of extra grams with them to make sure they wouldn't be short." Both of Mark's eyebrows raised as several wrinkles creased the middle of his forehead.

"So, you think I've been dipping in the packages?" Mark asked not wanting to think Ty had doubts about his loyalty to him.

"Nah, kid, but I got a feeling who it is though," Ty informed him as he ran his plan to catch whoever hand had been dipping in the cookie jar.

Within two days Ty had found out who'd been stealing off of the packages he had Mark and Alex delivering for him. Ty had no doubt that it wasn't Mark, since his money had never come up short in the entire year that he had been running for him.

Ty Called Mark and told him to bring Alex with him. His instructions were to meet Ty at an old tobacco warehouse by Adams School. "A yo, is there something you need to tell me before we get to the warehouse?" Mark asked, wondering if Alex had anything to do with the missing dope.

"Do you have to ask that?" Mark looked over at his brother.

"You right." He gave his brother a pound. "I had to ask." When Mark pulled up to the warehouse door, they slowly slid apart and he drove in. He suddenly felt a strange chill run up and down his spine when the door closed behind them. The headlights beamed on two figures across the room from them. They could make out the figure standing up and knew it was Ty, but the figure in the chair in front of him was hard to make out. Ty waved them over, so Mark drove closer. When he was directly in front of

Ty, the person in the chair became clear. It was

Jun-Bug. He was tied down and badly beaten.

"Get out, my friends," Ty demanded with an

evil grin on his face. This time Ty calling them

his friends didn't sound as good as it sounded

when they were at the club. For the first time

Mark wondered how much of a friend he was to

Ty. "Y'all remember ole Jun-Bug here,

don'tcha?" Ty asked, patting Jun-Bug on the

side of his face with his left hand and then

immediately following up with a right cross

sending Jun-Bug and the chair he sat in

crashing to the floor. "Pick this piece of shit up,"

he ordered Kessey, who came over and did as

was ordered.

"Come on, Cuz, help me," Jun-Bug pleaded with his older cousin Kessey. Kessey turned his head and walked away as Ty stood back over him.

"Shut the fuck up, nigga," Ty demanded with a sharp hook to Jun-Bug's ribs.

Mark's face balled up as he heard the sound of bones cracking. "You should've thought about the consequences before you decided to bite the hand that was feeding you, stupid ass." Mark and Alex stood there looking at Jun-Bug as he fought to keep his swollen eyes open. They began to wonder if Ty was going to kill him or not, and most importantly, if he was, why did he call them to watch? "This is what happens to a motherfucka that crosses me." Ty drew back his fist, ready to strike again. Jun-Bug flinched so hard he almost fell out of the chair, but it was too late. Ty hit him in his eye, closing it completely. Ty was sending a message to all of them, and they heard it loud and clear. He reached behind his back a pulled out a MAC-11 and an Uzi sub-machine gun. He pointed the barrels at Mark and Alex, and in one swift motion turned the handles toward them. They both looked at him confused, not wanting to make any sudden moves. "Here, take them." They took the guns from him and checked the clips. They were both filled to the top. "Are y'all down with me?" They both knew what Ty was asking them at that

point. Mark and Alex had never killed anyone

before. The room was silent for a few seconds

before the three-round burst from the Uzi filled

the air. Mark looked at his brother, and it was at

that very moment he knew Alex was natural-

born killer. He showed no emotions, no remorse

at all at the dead body before him. Ty didn't

expect Mark to pull the trigger. He knew he was

a hustler at heart, not a killer. The whole point of

Ty telling him to bring Alex along with him was

to see if he had the heart to really kill if the

moment ever presented itself. They both passed

the final test. After everything was done they

handed Ty back the guns, but he declined. "Go

ahead and keep them. Y'all deserve them. I'll be delivering them personally from here on out to make sure nothing like this ever happens again. Y'all cool with dat?" They agreed. He handed them two thousand apiece and then signaled for Kessey to clean up his cousin's remains and torch the place. On the way out, Mark and Kessey exchanged stares, and the look in Kessey's eyes let Mark know it wouldn't be long before they bumped heads. Alex felt the vibe and pointed his fingers like he was aiming a gun in Kessey's direction, then jerked his hand as if letting two shots off at him.

The ride home was made in complete silence. They were both lost in their own thoughts. Mark was thinking about all the money they were now making and whether it was worth someone losing their life. Alex's mind, on the other hand, was in a totally different zone. He was thinking about the feeling he felt when he let off the three-round burst from the Uzi that lay in his lap and wondered who was going to be the next victim on his long list of people that had crossed him and his brother in the past.

~ ~ ~

Before they made it across town, a thought crossed Alex's mind. "Yo, make the next right." He pointed at the corner up ahead. The first person Mark and Alex saw when they turned on Bragg Street was the one and only Big Kev.

"Perfect," Alex smiled, seeing that none of his other homies was with him. "Pull up on that clown," Alex ordered, ready to put in more work. Being that no one knew that Mark had copped a whip, it was easy for them to creep up on Big Kev.

When Big Kev served his customer, he looked up and saw a black car pulling over to the curb. "Hurry up. What you need?" he asked as he reached in his briefs to pull out the bag of crack he had hidden underneath his pants. When the window came completely down, Kev made the mistake of sticking his head inside the car.

CRACK

Alex struck him over his right eye, creating a large gash which blood began to flow freely from. "Ahhhh," Big Kev cried out in agony, losing his balance. By the time he regained his footing, it was too late. Mark and Alex were out of the car and on his ass in the blink of an eye.

When they were finally done, Big Kev was a bloody, unconscious mess. After kicking him a few more times, Mark and Alex jumped back in the car. As Mark put his car in drive, Alex reached out the window and let off a three-round burst from his Uzi. Frightened, D.J. stayed put, a half a block down the street between two abandoned houses, until Mark and Alex were out of sight. After seeing the big gun that Alex jumped out of the car with, there was no way

D.J. was going to pop off the little .380 he had

on him and risk getting killed.

~ ~ ~

"Yo, what happened?" Big Kev asked an

hour later once he came to.

"We don't know. We were hoping that you

could tell us," Rodney said hovering over Kev as

he lay on the couch. "D.J. found you laid out on

the sidewalk in front of the trap." Rodney looked

at D.J. then back to Kev.

"I-I-I don't remember," Big Kev stuttered. "All

I remember is someone pulling up on me in a

black car." He felt his pockets, only to find them

empty. "Yo, where my money and crack at?" he

asked dumbfounded. D.J. shrugged his shoulders and looked away, not wanting to look guilty of robbing his partner while he was knocked out cold.

"You sure you had it on you?" D.J. asked.

"What the fuck you think, nigga? I just said I was slanging out here earlier!"

"Don't get mad at me, Cuz. I wasn't them nigga's that went upside yo damn head." D.J. grinned slyly. Big Kev had just about enough of D.J.'s smart mouth.

"What the fuck you just say, lil nigga?" Big Kev jumped to his feet and headed over in D.J.'s direction, but Rodney stopped him from doing what he was planning on doing.

"Y'all two niggas chill the fuck out. We need to find out who had the balls to come to my shit and put hands on my homie," Rodney shouted, slamming his fist into the palm of his hand. Big Kev had a strange feeling that D.J. knew more than he was letting on. He prayed for his partner that he didn't.

"How else did he know it was more than one person?" He did say, "Them niggas," didn't he, Kev thought to himself.

"I need for you two to get out there and put y'all's ears to the streets and find out who is behind this shit," Rodney ordered. Without hesitation, Big Kev and D.J. headed for the door.

"Not you." Rodney stopped Big Kev in his tracks.

"Clean yourself up first." Big Kev looked down at his bloody clothes. Lucky for him, he always kept spare clothes in the back room to change into. The entire time Big Kev was in the back getting himself together, all that ran through his head was the comment D.J. made about his attackers.

"How did he know that it was more than one person?" he asked himself over and over again.

"If I find out that D.J. knows more than he's letting on, I'ma kill him and his cousin," Big Kev concluded as he walked out of the back room and down the hall.

8

WHEN IT RAINS, IT POURS

Mark finished his runs a little earlier that day
than he expected, so he dropped Alex off over
Torya's crib and headed to the arcade to meet
the love of his life. He figured he'd shoot a few
games of pool and win a couple of dollars from
the so-called pool sharks before Tosha arrived.

He parked his Legend in front of the arcade,
so he could keep a close eye on it. As soon as
he armed his alarm and turned around, he was
bum-rushed by two thirsty neighborhood

hoodrats. After taking their numbers with a promise that he would tear their backs out later, they finally let him go in the arcade. "Damn, these bitches wild," he said to himself thinking of all they just said they were going to do to him if he kept his promise. He made sure he locked their numbers in and put five stars behind their names and made a mental note to holla on the next rainy day. He just hoped it rained soon.

As soon as he walked in, the first person he saw was Tosha, but what made him stop in his tracks was the guy standing in front of her. His heart started beating at an alarming rate. Even from behind he could tell who it was, but when he turned to the side and he saw the side of his face, he knew it was Killa Mike.

Killa Mike was a serious threat to be reckoned with around Wilson. Even though he was only a few years older than Mark and only stood about five foot nine and weight 150 pounds soaking wet, it didn't change the fact that he held down one of the roughest neighborhoods in the city. He wore a deep scar on the side of his face that ran down to his neck, which told a story of its own. The word on the streets was that Killa Mike was the only one alive that could actually tell the story of that brutal blood bath, or at least he was the only one ever to mention what happened after four ruthless gangsters ended up dead in a drug deal gone wrong with him being the only survivor.

Mark really wasn't too worried about the hype because he had rumbled with the best of them and had come up on top. If he didn't win he earned their respect, especially after coming back with Alex. What really pushed him over the edge was the way Tosha was laughing and smiling. He had never seen her as happy, besides with him, but what really was the icing on the cake was when he saw Killa Mike hand her a wad of money. Mark looked around the arcade and began to notice people beginning to point and silently whisper in his direction. Turning around and walking out was no longer an option. He had to maintain the rep he'd earned because he knew once he let one buster slide others would be willing to test his gangster, and he couldn't have that. Besides, his pride wouldn't let him leave. He checked his clip and took his gun off safety and then tucked it back into his waistline. Not ever shooting anybody before had Mark a little on edge, but it was little too late to let what-ifs get in the way now. Mark made his way through the video games and the crowd of kids until he ended up directly behind Killa Mike. Mark tapped him on the shoulder. "Wassup, motherfucka?" Mark asked. Killa Mike turned around and was face-to-face with the barrel of Mark's MAC-11. The thing that scared Mark the most was the smile he got from Killa

Mike instead of fear. At that moment Mark wished he would've followed his first instinct and just walked out the door, and what confirmed it was when Killa Mike spoke.

"Nigga, you better pull that trigger, because if you don't, I will." Then he reached for his gun. Before he could pull it out Mark had no choice but to begin pumping him full of hot led.

"Mark," Tosha shouted. "Mark. Mark. Did you hear me? This is my brother, Michael." Tosha calling Mark's name snapped him out of his daydream.

"Damn, that shit seemed so real." He thought to shake Killa Mike's hand, but Killa Mike just stared at him.

"Don't I know you from somewhere?" Killa Mike asked as he began to search through his memory bank trying to place where he knew Mark from.

"I don't think so," Mark replied nervously because he knew Killa Mike very well. He just hoped he didn't remember him, at least not right now. Every now and then Ty would send him over to Killa Mike's spot to drop off a package or two whenever his connect was out of town or if there was a drought. There was no way he was going to remind him since he had yet to tell Tosha what his source of income was. She believed him when he told her that he was a delivery boy, which was true. She just thought

173

the delivery was groceries instead of drugs. He definitely didn't want her to find out that way. He just hoped Killa Mike didn't blow his cover. To his surprise, Killa Mike didn't say anything, even though he gave him a look like he knew where he remembered him from, and his last statement confirmed it.

"Yo, kid, my sister can't have no boyfriend." Those words felt like a Mack Truck had just crashed into Mark's chest. He would've rather Killa Mike just told Tosha what he did for a living. To make sure Mark knew he was serious, he leaned in and whispered in his ear, "And if I catch you anywhere around my sister again you are gonna personally feel why I got this name. I don't care who you work for, lil nigga." Tosha's

smile faded. She could tell by the serious look

on Mark's face that whatever Killa Mike was

saying couldn't have been anything good.

Before she could say anything to find out what

was going on, Killa Mike cut her off. "Go get in

my truck," he demanded while pointing at the

tricked-out Escalade out front parked in front of

Mark's Acura. She knew by the tone of his voice

that there was nothing she could say to change

his mind, so she just lowered her head,

embarrassed as everyone cleared the way for

her to make it to the door. As she opened it she

took one last look back at the two loves of her

life as the tears ran down her cheeks. Mark

wanted to explain himself, but after that look Killa Mike gave him, he decided against it. Killa Mike walked away, never turning his back on Mark knowing that he was packing heat as well. He had learned a valuable lesson from the last time he did that. It almost cost him his life along with a hundred and fifty grand.

As Mark drove home all he could think about was the look in Tosha's eyes. He wondered if it was over between them. He wanted to be mad at Killa Mike, but he couldn't be because he would've reacted the same way, if not worse, if it happened to his own sister. As a matter of fact, him and Alex had fucked up a couple of guys for less. He tried to rationalize the situation since his reason for hustling was different than a lot of hustlers', but he quickly erased that because a hustler was a hustler no matter the reason.

Mark parked his car in front of his apartment building. He repeatedly slammed his fist against his steering wheel and shouted, "How could I have been so stupid?" His heart ached for Tosha, and it was then he realized that what Alex and Ty always teased him about was true. He was in love with Tosha, and he knew that she was in love with him as well, and now she had been taken away from him. They had never even had sex before, so he knew that wasn't the reason he was feeling the way he was feeling about her. He rapidly blinked his eyes trying to fight back the floodgate of tears that were threatening to fall, and when he was no longer able to stop them, they came down fast and steady.

Mark made his way into the house and hit his mother and sister off with some pocket change and then headed to his room to try to get some rest. He was glad Alex was down at Torya's crib because it was peaceful and quiet, and that was exactly what he needed. He definitely wasn't in the mood to be answering the twenty-one questions he was sure Alex would be asking him after seeing him in such a depressed state of mind.

He tried to figure out a way he could make

things right with her but kept coming up blank

because she already had everything a girl could

ever want. Then it finally hit him. "I'll send her

some flowers and a poem tomorrow," he

thought to himself as he pulled out a pad and

pen from his book bag. Poems were something

he did when he felt alone or had some things on

his mind. That was the best way he could

express himself without being judged by people.

"Roses are red, and violets are blue." He

burst out into laughter and balled the piece of

paper up and threw it in the trash. "Nah, I gotta

come from the heart with this one." He turned

the radio to the Quiet Storm. They were playing

"Moments in Love" by the Art of Noise, and the

words seemed to come from everywhere.

'Love

Love can bring pleasure, Love can bring pain. Love can make you so happy, also drive you insane. So, once you find Love, cherish it, keep your feelings in the light. Do whatever to show you care, do whatever to make things right, because once it's damaged, it's hard to repair. No one said Love was honest, no one said love was fair. Love is caring, Love is sharing, Love is built on a thing called trust, Love is kind, although Love is blind, but in the best of times,
Love was us!'

After he was finished writing, he lay back on his bed and thought about all the fun times they shared together, and before he knew it he had dozed off.

A few weeks went by, and even though he hadn't seen or heard from her, he had thought about her every day. He felt it was only right to give her her space out of respect for her and her brother. It was killing him not to see his better half.

On a Friday around noon, Mark and Alex were sitting on the stoop in front of their apartment building waiting on Ty to come and bring them the packages he needed delivered that day. Mark never told Alex about the run-in he had with Killa Mike at the arcade that day, but Ty arrived and informed them that his spot was one of the places he needed them to visit. He knew he could no longer keep it a secret just in case Killa Mike felt some type of way.

They made the first two runs in silence. On the way to the third and final spot, Alex noticed something was worrying Mark. "Yo, Bruh." Mark turned his head to see what Alex wanted. "What's on your mind? You haven't been yourself in the past few days." Alex had learned in the short time they'd been in the game that emotions could be ranked at the top of a person's downfall, right under jealously. Mark knew he had to tell his brother what was on his mind.

"It's Tosha," Mark responded dryly.

"What's the matter? She still ain't gave you the panty draws yet?" Alex asked jokingly. After he saw that Mark wasn't laughing along with him, he became serious.

"Nah, man, it ain't that."

"So, you did finally hit?" Alex asked, waiting to hear the full details.

"I didn't say that." Now Alex was getting annoyed.

"Well, what is it?"

"I'll tell you if you shut up and listen!" Alex sat quietly as Mark ran down the arcade situation to him. "It's her brother. He don't want her seeing me anymore."

"Man, fuck her brother. He can't control who she go out with." Mark looked at Alex with a look on his face that reminded him that they were the same way about Nicole. "Yeah, you got a point there." Mark put his eyes back on the road as Alex fired off question after question. "So who is her brother, anyway?" Mark took a deep breath hoping Alex was ready for the bombshell that he was about to drop on him.

"Killa Mike."

"The Killa Mike?"

Mark nodded his head up and down.

"The nigga we 'bout to go serve?"

"Yep." Mark thought that Alex would be upset for not telling him earlier, but all he did was check his clip and say fuck it.

"So, what you gonna do about Tosha?" Alex asked.

"What can I do?" Alex didn't know the answer to that question himself, so he said nothing. "I guess I'll just wait until she decides to call."

"She might not ever call if her brother decides to act a fool once we get over here," Alex said with a smirk on his face as he patted the Uzi on his lap. Mark hoped like hell that it didn't have to result to that, but like he was always told, "You'd rather be judged by twelve

185

than carried by six." Mark felt like he had the bubble guts as he turned the corner to Killa Mike's block. "Here goes nothing." Alex put a bullet in the chamber preparing for the worst.

"Chill, Bruh, let me do all the talking, and I'm sure we won't have to resort to that." Mark looked over at Alex hoping that he was listening, but the look on Alex's face was hard to read.

Killa Mike's trap house was the very last house on a dead-end street with a tall fence around it. He had two large pits running around freely in the yard, which made it hard for police to do a sneak attack, or anybody else for that matter.

As soon as Mark and Alex exited the car, the

two pits ran to the fence and began biting it as if they were trying to pull it down to get to them. They quickly jumped back and reached for their straps. Mark grabbed his cell from his pocket and was about to call Ty and let him know their situation. "Sit, Diamond, sit Pearl," Killa Mike yelled from the doorway, and just like that the biting at the fence as well as the growling stopped. "Come on in." Mark and Alex looked at each other and then to Killa Mike like he was crazy. "They're harmless," Killa Mike said with a grin then clapped his hands together twice. The pits immediately stood to their feet and trotted to the back yard without looking back. Mark was the first to enter the fence, followed by Alex.

They both kept their eyes trained on the side of the house with their hands ready to grab their gats just in case the dogs tried to do a sneak attack.

They followed Killa Mike into a large kitchen. On the table was a digital scale, used razors, a jar with about a quarter ounce of residue in it, a few baggies, and a microwave. "You gonna stand around and look, or are y'all gonna handle business? I ain't got all day," Killa Mike said, letting them know he wanted them out as soon as possible. Mark handed him the book bag and waited patiently for him to scan through the product. Killa Mike nodded in approval and then handed Mark the envelope. "Ay, kid, let me holla at your brother in private for a second," Mike

demanded to Alex. Alex wasn't feeling his tone

and was about to speak on it until Mark cut in.

"Everything good, Bruh."

"You sure?"

"I'm sure." Alex nodded his head and walked

out the front door to the car. He wasn't feeling

Mark's choice, but what could he do? He kept

the music off and the window down just in case

he heard anything out of the ordinary come from

the house.

Once they were all alone Killa Mike turned

his attention to Mark. "Yo, playboy, I want you to

know that I don't got no beef with you, so you

can take that tough-guy look off your face." Mark

could tell that Killa Mike was trying to intimidate him. "You seem like a cool kid, but when it comes down to my little sister and who she dates, I only got her best interest in mind. You must be a good dude because every day I hear Tosha on the phone crying to one of her little girlfriends about how much she misses you." That made Mark light up on the inside, but he kept a straight face. He also felt a little sad because he was the reason for her feeling so down. "I called Ty for some work 'cause I knew he would send you and I wanted to talk to you without Tosha finding out. I want you to think about the road you have chosen to take and think about my sister and how this road can also affect her life." Mark had been thinking about the same exact thing for the past few weeks already. Just as he was about to explain his reasons for hustling, Killa Mike cut him off. "You don't have to explain anything to me, just think about what I just said." Mark agreed, and after they dapped each other up, Mark turned around and headed for the front door. "Oh, I almost forgot." Mark stopped and turned back around. "Nice poem." They both smiled, and Mark turned back around feeling kind of embarrassed. He wondered how Killa Mike knew that he had written Tosha a poem and if that was why he had called him over to talk to him.

As soon as Mark got in the car, Alex began

with the questions. "So, what the nigga want to talk to you in private about?" Mark told him everything that was said between the two, mostly what Killa Mike had said since all he did was nod his head. "So, what the fuck you smiling for, nigga?"

"Nothing," was all he said as he made a U-turn in the street and sped off. There was no way he was going to tell Alex about the poem. He knew he'd never hear the end of it, and he didn't want to ruin the good feeling he had right now that things weren't truly over between him and Tosha.

TO BE CONTINUED...

Text Good2Go at 31996 to receive new Release updates via text message.

To order books, please fill out the order form below:
To order films please go to www.good2gofilms.com
Name: __ _____
Address:_____
City: _____ State: _____ Zip Code: _____
Phone:_____
Email:_____
Method of Payment: Check   VISA   MASTERCARD
Credit Card#:_ _____
Name as it appears on card: _____
Signature: _____

Item Name	Price	Qty	Amount
48 Hours to Die – Silk White	$14.99		
A Hustler's Dream - Ernest Morris	$14.99		
A Hustler's Dream 2 - Ernest Morris	$14.99		
A Thug's Devotion – J. L. Rose and J. M. McMillon	$14.99		
All Eyes on Tommy Gunz – Warren Holloway	$14.99		
Black Reign – Ernest Morris	$14.99		
Bloody Mayhem Down South – Trayvon Jackson	$14.99		
Bloody Mayhem Down South 2 – Trayvon Jackson	$14.99		
Business Is Business – Silk White	$14.99		
Business Is Business 2 – Silk White	$14.99		
Business Is Business 3 – Silk White	$14.99		
Cash In Cash Out – Assa Raymond Baker	$14.99		
Cash In Cash Out 2 - Assa Raymond Baker	$14.99		
Childhood Sweethearts – Jacob Spears	$14.99		
Childhood Sweethearts 2 – Jacob Spears	$14.99		
Childhood Sweethearts 3 - Jacob Spears	$14.99		
Childhood Sweethearts 4 - Jacob Spears	$14.99		
Connected To The Plug – Dwan Marquis Williams	$14.99		
Connected To The Plug 2 – Dwan Marquis Williams	$14.99		
Connected To The Plug 3 – Dwan Williams	$14.99		
Deadly Reunion – Ernest Morris	$14.99		
Dream's Life – Assa Raymond Baker	$14.99		

Flipping Numbers – Ernest Morris	$14.99		
Flipping Numbers 2 – Ernest Morris	$14.99		
He Loves Me, He Loves You Not - Mychea	$14.99		
He Loves Me, He Loves You Not 2 - Mychea	$14.99		
He Loves Me, He Loves You Not 3 - Mychea	$14.99		
He Loves Me, He Loves You Not 4 – Mychea	$14.99		
He Loves Me, He Loves You Not 5 – Mychea	$14.99		
Kings of the Block – Dwan Willams	$14.99		
Kings of the Block 2 – Dwan Willams	$14.99		
Lord of My Land – Jay Morrison	$14.99		
Lost and Turned Out – Ernest Morris	$14.99		
Love Hates Violence – De'Wayne Maris	$14.99		
Married To Da Streets – Silk White	$14.99		
M.E.R.C. - Make Every Rep Count Health and Fitness	$14.99		
Money Make Me Cum – Ernest Morris	$14.99		
My Besties – Asia Hill	$14.99		
My Besties 2 – Asia Hill	$14.99		
My Besties 3 – Asia Hill	$14.99		
My Besties 4 – Asia Hill	$14.99		
My Boyfriend's Wife - Mychea	$14.99		
My Boyfriend's Wife 2 – Mychea	$14.99		
My Brothers Envy – J. L. Rose	$14.99		
My Brothers Envy 2 – J. L. Rose	$14.99		
Naughty Housewives – Ernest Morris	$14.99		
Naughty Housewives 2 – Ernest Morris	$14.99		
Naughty Housewives 3 – Ernest Morris	$14.99		
Naughty Housewives 4 – Ernest Morris	$14.99		
Never Be The Same – Silk White	$14.99		
Shades of Revenge – Assa Raymond Baker	$14.99		
Slumped – Jason Brent	$14.99		
Someone's Gonna Get It – Mychea	$14.99		

Stranded – Silk White	$14.99		
Supreme & Justice – Ernest Morris	$14.99		
Supreme & Justice 2 – Ernest Morris	$14.99		
Supreme & Justice 3 – Ernest Morris	$14.99		
Tears of a Hustler - Silk White	$14.99		
Tears of a Hustler 2 - Silk White	$14.99		
Tears of a Hustler 3 - Silk White	$14.99		
Tears of a Hustler 4- Silk White	$14.99		
Tears of a Hustler 5 – Silk White	$14.99		
Tears of a Hustler 6 – Silk White	$14.99		
The Last Love Letter – Warren Holloway	$14.99		
The Last Love Letter 2 – Warren Holloway	$14.99		
The Panty Ripper - Reality Way	$14.99		
The Panty Ripper 3 – Reality Way	$14.99		
The Solution – Jay Morrison	$14.99		
The Teflon Queen – Silk White	$14.99		
The Teflon Queen 2 – Silk White	$14.99		
The Teflon Queen 3 – Silk White	$14.99		
The Teflon Queen 4 – Silk White	$14.99		
The Teflon Queen 5 – Silk White	$14.99		
The Teflon Queen 6 - Silk White	$14.99		
The Vacation – Silk White	$14.99		
Tied To A Boss - J.L. Rose	$14.99		
Tied To A Boss 2 - J.L. Rose	$14.99		
Tied To A Boss 3 - J.L. Rose	$14.99		
Tied To A Boss 4 - J.L. Rose	$14.99		
Tied To A Boss 5 - J.L. Rose	$14.99		
Time Is Money - Silk White	$14.99		
Tomorrow's Not Promised – Robert Torres	$14.99		
Tomorrow's Not Promised 2 – Robert Torres	$14.99		
Two Mask One Heart – Jacob Spears and Trayvon Jackson	$14.99		

Two Mask One Heart 2 – Jacob Spears and Trayvon Jackson	$14.99		
Two Mask One Heart 3 – Jacob Spears and Trayvon Jackson	$14.99		
Wrong Place Wrong Time – Silk White	$14.99		
Young Goonz – Reality Way	$14.99		
Subtotal:			
Tax:			
Shipping (Free) U.S. Media Mail:			
Total:			

Make Checks Payable To:
Good2Go Publishing
7311 W Glass Lane,
Laveen, AZ 85339

CPSIA information can be obtained
at www.ICGtesting.com
Printed in the USA
LVHW011925010419
612564LV00017B/209

9 781947 340350